Dark Reunion

Volume IV

L. J. Smith

HarperTorch
An Imprint of HarperCollins*Publishers*

This is a work of fiction. Names, characters, places, and incidents are products of the author's imagination or are used fictitiously and are not to be construed as real. Any resemblance to actual events, locales, organizations, or persons, living or dead, is entirely coincidental.

HARPERTORCH
An Imprint of HarperCollins*Publishers*
10 East 53rd Street
New York, New York 10022-5299

ISBN: 0-06-105992-7

First HarperTorch paperback printing: October 2001
First HarperPrism printing: April 1999

A mass market edition of this book was published in 1992 by HarperPaperbacks.

Produced by Daniel Weiss Associates, Inc., 33 West 17th Street, New York, NY 10011.

Printed in the United States of America

Visit HarperTorch on the World Wide Web at
www.harpercollins.com

10 9 8 7 6 5 4 3

For John and Marianne Vrabec, with love.
And with thanks to Julie—again—for
helping it get written.

Message from the other side . . .

"Come on, Elena," Bonnie whispered. "Talk to me."

The planchette began to move.

None of them could be guiding it; they were all applying pressure from different points. Bonnie kept her eyes shut until it stopped and then looked. The planchette was pointing to the word *Yes.*

Suddenly Bonnie's heart was beating so hard she was afraid it would shake her fingers. "I wanted to talk to you, but things got weird—"

THERE ARE BAD THINGS VERY BAD THINGS OUT HERE

"Like what?" Bonnie leaned closer to the board.

YOU NEED HELP HE'S OUT OF YOUR LEAGUE NOW LISTEN AND FOLLOW INSTRUCTIONS—

Without warning, the planchette jerked away from the letters and flew around the board wildly.

"Elena!" Bonnie was frightened. The planchette was pulsing with energy, a dark and ugly energy like boiling black tar that stung her fingers. But she could also feel the quivering silver thread that was Elena's presence fighting it. "Don't let go!" she cried desperately.

BONNIE GET OUT HES HERE RUN RUN RU—

The planchette jerked furiously, whipped out from under Bonnie's fingers and beyond her reach, flying across the board and through the air as if someone had thrown it.

And then all the lights went out, plunging the house into darkness.

BOOKS BY L. J. SMITH

THE VAMPIRE DIARIES

Volume I: The Awakening
Volume II: The Struggle
Volume III: The Fury
Volume IV: Dark Reunion

THE SECRET CIRCLE TRILOGY

Volume I: The Initiation
Volume II: The Captive
Volume III: The Power

The Night of the Solstice
Heart of Valor

Dark Reunion

One

"Things can be just like they were before," said Caroline warmly, reaching out to squeeze Bonnie's hand.

But it wasn't true. Nothing could ever be the way it had been before Elena died. Nothing. And Bonnie had serious misgivings about this party Caroline was trying to set up. A vague nagging in the pit of her stomach told her that for some reason it was a very, very bad idea.

"Meredith's birthday is already *over*," she pointed out. "It was last Saturday."

"But she didn't have a party, not a real party like this one. We've got all night; my parents won't be back until Sunday morning. Come on, Bonnie—just think how surprised she'll be."

Oh, she'll be surprised, all right, thought Bonnie. So surprised she just might kill me afterward. "Look, Caroline, the reason Meredith didn't have a big party is that she still doesn't feel much like celebrating. It seems—disrespectful, somehow—"

"But that's *wrong*. Elena would want us to have a good time, you know she would. She loved parties. And she'd hate to see us sitting around and crying over her six months after she's gone." Caroline leaned forward, her normally feline green eyes earnest and compelling. There was no artifice in them now, none of Caroline's usual nasty manipulation. Bonnie could tell she really meant it.

"I want us to be friends again the way we used to be," Caroline said. "We always used to celebrate our birthdays together, just the four of us, remember? And remember how the guys would always try to crash our parties? I wonder if they'll try this year."

Bonnie felt control of the situation slipping away from her. This is a bad idea, this is a very bad idea, she thought. But Caroline was going on, looking dreamy and almost romantic as she talked about the good old days. Bonnie didn't have the heart to tell her that the good old days were as dead as disco.

"But there aren't even four of us anymore. Three doesn't make much of a party," she protested feebly when she could get a word in.

"I'm going to invite Sue Carson, too. Meredith gets along with her, doesn't she?"

Bonnie had to admit Meredith did; everyone got along with Sue. But even so, Caroline had to understand that things couldn't be the way they had been before. You couldn't just substitute Sue Carson for Elena and say, There, everything is fixed now.

But how do I explain that to Caroline? Bonnie thought. Suddenly she knew.

"Let's invite Vickie Bennett," she said.

Caroline stared. "*Vickie Bennett?* You must be joking. Invite that bizarre little drip who undressed in front of half the school? After everything that happened?"

"*Because* of everything that happened," said Bonnie firmly. "Look, I know she was never in our crowd. But she's not in with the fast crowd anymore; they don't want her and she's scared to death of them. She needs friends. We need people. Let's invite her."

For a moment Caroline looked helplessly frustrated. Bonnie thrust her chin out, put her hands on her hips, and waited. Finally Caroline sighed.

"All right; you win. I'll invite her. But you have to take care of getting Meredith to my house Saturday night. And Bonnie—make sure she doesn't have any idea what's going on. I really want this to be a surprise."

"Oh, it will be," Bonnie said grimly. She was unprepared for the sudden light in Caroline's face or the impulsive warmth of Caroline's hug.

"I'm so glad you're seeing things my way," Caroline said. "And it'll be so good for us all to be together again."

She doesn't understand a thing, Bonnie realized, dazed, as Caroline walked off. What do I have to do to explain to her? Sock her?

And then: Oh, God, now I have to tell Meredith.

But by the end of the day she decided that maybe Meredith didn't need to be told. Caroline wanted Meredith surprised; well, maybe Bonnie should deliver Meredith surprised. That way at least Meredith wouldn't have to worry about it beforehand. Yes, Bonnie concluded, it was probably kindest to *not* tell Meredith anything.

And who knows, she wrote in her journal Friday night. *Maybe I'm being too hard on Caroline. Maybe she's really sorry about all the things she did to us, like trying to humiliate Elena in front of the whole town and trying to get Stefan put away for murder. Maybe Caroline's matured since then and learned to think about somebody besides herself. Maybe we'll actually have a good time at her party.*

And maybe aliens will kidnap me before tomorrow afternoon, she thought as she closed the diary. She could only hope.

The diary was an inexpensive drugstore blank book, with a pattern of tiny flowers on the cover. She'd only started keeping it since Elena had died, but she'd already become slightly addicted to it. It was the one place she could say anything she wanted without people looking shocked and saying, "Bonnie McCullough!" or "Oh, *Bonnie*."

She was still thinking about Elena as she turned off the light and crawled under the covers.

She was sitting on lush, manicured grass that spread as far as she could see in all directions. The sky was a flawless blue, the air was warm and scented. Birds were singing.

"I'm so glad you could come," Elena said.

"Oh—yes," said Bonnie. "Well, naturally, so am I. Of course." She looked around again, then hastily back at Elena.

"More tea?"

There was a teacup in Bonnie's hand, thin and fragile as eggshell. "Oh—sure. Thanks."

Elena was wearing an eighteenth-century dress of gauzy white muslin, which clung to her, showing how slender she was. She poured the tea precisely, without spilling a drop.

"Would you like a mouse?"

"A *what*?"

"I said, would you like a sandwich with your tea?"

"Oh. A sandwich. Yeah. Great." It was thinly sliced cucumber with mayonnaise on a dainty square of white bread. Without the crust.

The whole scene was as sparkly and beautiful as a picture by Seurat. Warm Springs, that's where we are. The old picnic place, Bonnie thought. But surely we've got more important things to discuss than tea.

"Who does your hair these days?" she asked. Elena never had been able to do it herself.

"Do you like it?" Elena put a hand up to the silky, pale gold mass piled at the back of her neck.

"It's perfect," said Bonnie, sounding for all the world like her mother at a Daughters of the American Revolution dinner party.

"Well, hair is important, you know," Elena said. Her eyes glowed a deeper blue than the sky, lapis lazuli blue. Bonnie touched her own springy red curls self-consciously.

"Of course, blood is important too," Elena said.

"Blood? Oh—yes, of course," said Bonnie, flustered. She had no idea what Elena was talking about, and she felt as if she were walking on a tightrope over alligators. "Yes, blood's important, all right," she agreed weakly.

"Another sandwich?"

"Thanks." It was cheese and tomato. Elena selected one for herself and bit into it delicately. Bonnie watched her, feeling uneasiness grow by the minute inside her, and then—

And then she saw the mud oozing out of the edges of the sandwich.

"What—*what's that?*" Terror made her voice shrill. For the first time, the dream seemed like a dream, and she found that she couldn't move, could only gasp and stare. A thick glob of the brown stuff fell off Elena's sandwich onto the checkered tablecloth. It was mud, all right. "Elena . . . Elena, what—"

"Oh, we all eat this down here." Elena smiled at her with brown-stained teeth. Except that the voice wasn't Elena's; it was ugly and distorted and it was a man's voice. "You will too."

The air was no longer warm and scented; it was hot and sickly sweet with the odor of rotting garbage. There were black pits in the green grass, which wasn't manicured after all but wild and overgrown. This wasn't Warm Springs. She was in the old graveyard; how could she not have realized that? Only these graves were fresh.

"Another mouse?" Elena said, and giggled obscenely.

Bonnie looked down at the half-eaten sandwich she was holding and screamed. Dangling from one end was a ropy brown tail. She threw it as hard as she could against a headstone, where it hit with a wet slap. Then she stood, stomach heaving, scrubbing her fingers frantically against her jeans.

"You can't leave yet. The company is just arriving." Elena's face was changing; she had already lost her hair, and her skin was turning gray and leathery. Things were moving in the plate of sandwiches and the freshly dug pits. Bonnie didn't want to see any of them; she thought she would go mad if she did.

"You're not Elena!" she screamed, and ran.

The wind blew her hair into her eyes and she couldn't see. Her pursuer was behind her; she could feel it right behind her. Get to the bridge, she thought, and then she ran into something.

"I've been waiting for you," said the thing in Elena's dress, the gray skeletal thing with long, twisted teeth. "Listen to me, Bonnie." It held her with terrible strength.

"You're not Elena! You're not Elena!"

"Listen to me, Bonnie!"

It was Elena's voice, Elena's real voice, not obscenely amused nor thick and ugly, but urgent. It came from somewhere behind Bonnie and it swept through the dream like a fresh, cold wind. "Bonnie, listen quickly—"

Things were melting. The bony hands on

Bonnie's arms, the crawling graveyard, the rancid hot air. For a moment Elena's voice was clear, but it was broken up like a bad long-distance connection.

". . . He's twisting things, changing them. I'm not as strong as he is . . ." Bonnie missed some words. ". . . but this is important. You have to find . . . right now." Her voice was fading.

"Elena, I can't hear you! Elena!"

". . . an easy spell, only two ingredients, the ones I told you already . . ."

"Elena!"

Bonnie was still shouting as she sat bolt upright in bed.

Two

"And that's all I remember," Bonnie concluded as she and Meredith walked down Sunflower Street between the rows of tall Victorian houses.

"But it was definitely Elena?"

"Yes, and she was trying to tell me something at the end. But that's the part that wasn't clear, except that it was important, terribly important. What do you think?"

"Mouse sandwiches and open graves?" Meredith arched an elegant eyebrow. "I think you're getting Stephen King mixed up with Lewis Carroll."

Bonnie thought she was probably right. But the dream still bothered her; it had bothered her all day, enough to put her earlier worries out of her mind. Now, as she and Meredith approached

Caroline's house, the old worries returned with a vengeance.

She really should have told Meredith about this, she thought, casting an uneasy sideways glance at the taller girl. She shouldn't let Meredith just walk in there unprepared. . . .

Meredith looked up at the lighted windows of the Queen Anne House with a sigh. "Do you really *need* those earrings tonight?"

"Yes, I do; yes, absolutely." Too late now. Might as well make the best of it. "You'll love them when you see them," she added, hearing the note of hopeful desperation in her own voice.

Meredith paused and her keen dark eyes searched Bonnie's face curiously. Then she knocked on the door. "I just hope Caroline's not staying home tonight. We could end up stuck with her."

"Caroline staying home on a Saturday night? Don't be ridiculous." Bonnie had been holding her breath too long; she was starting to feel lightheaded. Her tinkling laughter came out brittle and false. "What a concept," she continued somewhat hysterically as Meredith said, "I don't think *anybody's* home," and tried the knob. Possessed by some crazy impulse Bonnie added, "Fiddle-dee-dee."

Hand on doorknob, Meredith stopped dead and turned to look at her.

"Bonnie," she said quietly, "have you gone completely through the ozone?"

"No." Deflated, Bonnie grabbed Meredith's arm and sought her eyes urgently. The door was opening on its own. "Oh, God, Meredith, please don't kill me . . ."

"*Surprise!*" shouted three voices.

"Smile," Bonnie hissed, shoving the suddenly resistant body of her friend through the door and into the bright room full of noise and showers of foil confetti. She beamed wildly herself and spoke through clenched teeth. "Kill me later—I deserve it—but for now just smile."

There were balloons, the expensive Mylar kind, and a cluster of presents on the coffee table. There was even a flower arrangement, although Bonnie noticed the orchids in it matched Caroline's pale green scarf exactly. It was a Hermes silk with a design of vines and leaves. She'll end up wearing one of those orchids in her hair, I'll bet, Bonnie thought.

Sue Carson's blue eyes were a little anxious, her smile wavering. "I hope you didn't have any big plans for tonight, Meredith," she said.

"Nothing I can't break with an iron crowbar," Meredith replied. But she smiled back with wry warmth and Bonnie relaxed. Sue had been a Homecoming Princess on Elena's court, along with Bonnie, Meredith, and Caroline. She was the only girl at school besides Bonnie and Meredith who'd stood by Elena when everyone else had turned against her. At Elena's funeral she'd said that Elena would always be the real queen of Robert E. Lee, and she'd given up her own nomination for Snow Queen in Elena's memory. Nobody could hate Sue. The worst was over now, Bonnie thought.

"I want to get a picture of us all on the couch," Caroline said, positioning them behind the flower arrangement. "Vickie, take it, will you?"

Vickie Bennett had been standing by quietly, unnoticed. Now she said, "Oh, sure," and nervously flicked long, light brown hair out of her eyes as she picked up the camera.

Just like she's some kind of servant, Bonnie thought, and then the flashbulb blinded her.

As the Polaroid developed and Sue and Caroline laughed and talked around Meredith's dry politeness, Bonnie noticed something else. It was a good picture; Caroline looked stunning as ever with her auburn hair gleaming and the pale green orchids in front of her. And there was Meredith, looking resigned and ironic and darkly beautiful without even trying, and there she was herself, a head shorter than the others, with her red curls tousled and a sheepish expression on her face. But the strange thing was the figure beside her on the couch. It was Sue, of course it was Sue, but for a moment the blond hair and blue eyes seemed to belong to someone else. Someone looking at her urgently, on the verge of saying something important. Bonnie frowned at the photo, blinking rapidly. The image swam in front of her, and a chilling uneasiness ran up her spine.

No, it was just Sue in the picture. She must've gone crazy for a minute, or else she was letting Caroline's desire for them "all to be together again" affect her.

"I'll take the next one," she said, springing up. "Sit down, Vickie, and lean in. No, farther, farther—there!" All of Vickie's movements were quick and light and nervous. When the flashbulb went off, she started like a scared animal ready to bolt.

Caroline scarcely glanced at this picture, getting up and heading for the kitchen instead. "Guess what we're having instead of cake?" she said. "I'm making my own version of Death by Chocolate. Come on, you've got to help me melt the fudge." Sue followed her, and after an uncertain pause, so did Vickie.

The last traces of Meredith's pleasant expression evaporated and she turned to Bonnie. "You should have told me."

"I know." Bonnie lowered her head meekly a minute. Then she looked up and grinned. "But then you wouldn't have come and we wouldn't be having Death by Chocolate."

"And that makes it all worthwhile?"

"Well, it helps," Bonnie said, with an air of being reasonable. "And really, it probably won't be so bad. Caroline's actually trying to be nice, and it's good for Vickie to get out of the house for once . . ."

"It doesn't look like it's good for her," Meredith said bluntly. "It looks like she's going to have a heart attack."

"Well, she's probably just nervous." In Bonnie's opinion, Vickie had good reason to be nervous. She'd spent most of the previous fall in a trance, being slowly driven out of her mind by a power she didn't understand. Nobody had expected her to come out of it as well as she had.

Meredith was still looking bleak. "At least," Bonnie said consolingly, "it isn't your real birthday."

Meredith picked up the camera and turned it over and over. Still looking down at her hands, she said, "But it is."

"What?" Bonnie stared and then said louder, "*What* did you say?"

"I said, it is my real birthday. Caroline's mom must have told her; she and my mom used to be friends a long time ago."

"Meredith, what are you talking about? Your birthday was last week, May 30."

"No, it wasn't. It's today, June 6. It's true; it's on my driver's license and everything. My parents started celebrating it a week early because June 6 was too upsetting for them. It was the day my grandfather was attacked and went crazy." As Bonnie gasped, unable to speak, she added calmly, "He tried to kill my grandmother, you know. He tried to kill me, too." Meredith put the camera down carefully in the exact center of the coffee table. "We really should go in the kitchen," she said quietly. "I smell chocolate."

Bonnie was still paralyzed, but her mind was beginning to work again. Vaguely, she remembered Meredith speaking about this before, but she hadn't told her the full truth then. And she hadn't said when it had happened.

"Attacked—you mean like Vickie was attacked," Bonnie got out. She couldn't say the word *vampire*, but she knew Meredith understood.

"Like Vickie was attacked," Meredith confirmed. "Come on," she added, even more quietly. "They're waiting for us. I didn't mean to upset you."

* * *

Meredith doesn't want me to be upset, so I *won't* be upset, Bonnie thought, pouring hot fudge over the chocolate cake and chocolate ice cream. Even though we've been friends since first grade and she never told me this secret before.

For an instant her skin chilled and words came floating out of the dark corners of her mind. *No one is what they seem.* She'd been warned that last year by the voice of Honoria Fell speaking through her, and the prophecy had turned out to be horrifyingly true. What if it wasn't over yet?

Then Bonnie shook her head determinedly. She couldn't think about this right now; she had a *party* to think about. And I'll make sure it's a *good* party and we all get along somehow, she thought.

Strangely, it wasn't even that hard. Meredith and Vickie didn't talk much at first, but Bonnie went out of her way to be nice to Vickie, and even Meredith couldn't resist the pile of brightly wrapped presents on the coffee table. By the time she'd opened the last one they were all talking and laughing. The mood of truce and toleration continued as they moved up into Caroline's bedroom to examine her clothes and CDs and photo albums. As it got near midnight they flopped on sleeping bags, still talking.

"What's going on with Alaric these days?" Sue asked Meredith.

Alaric Saltzman was Meredith's boyfriend—sort of. He was a graduate student from Duke University who'd majored in parapsychology and had been called to Fell's Church last year when the vampire attacks began. Though he'd started out an enemy, he'd ended up an ally—and a friend.

"He's in Russia," Meredith said. "Perestroika, you know? He's over there finding out what they were doing with psychics during the Cold War."

"What are you going to tell him when he gets back?" asked Caroline.

It was a question Bonnie would have liked to ask Meredith herself. Because Alaric was almost four years older, Meredith had told him to wait until after she graduated to talk about their future. But now Meredith was eighteen—today, Bonnie reminded herself—and graduation was in two weeks. What was going to happen after that?

"I haven't decided," Meredith said. "Alaric wants me to go to Duke, and I've been accepted there, but I'm not sure. I have to think."

Bonnie was just as glad. She wanted Meredith to go to Boone Junior College with *her*, not go off and get married, or even engaged. It was stupid to decide on one guy so young. Bonnie herself was notorious for playing the field, going from boy to boy as she pleased. She got crushes easily, and got over them just as easily.

"I haven't seen the guy so far worth remaining faithful to," she said now.

Everyone looked at her quickly. Sue's chin was resting on her fists as she asked, "Not even Stefan?"

Bonnie should have known. With the only light the dim bedside lamp and the only sound the rustle of new leaves on the weeping willows outside, it was inevitable that the conversation would turn to Stefan—and to Elena.

Stefan Salvatore and Elena Gilbert were already a sort of legend in the town, like Romeo and Juliet. When Stefan had first come to Fell's Church, every girl had wanted him. And Elena, the most beautiful, most popular, most unapproachable girl at school, had wanted him too. It was only after she'd gotten him that she realized the danger. Stefan wasn't what he seemed—he had a secret far darker than anyone could have guessed. And he had a brother, Damon, even more mysterious and dangerous than himself. Elena had been caught between the two brothers, loving Stefan but drawn irresistibly to Damon's wildness. In the end she had died to save them both, and to redeem their love.

"Maybe Stefan—if you're Elena," Bonnie murmured, yielding the point. The atmosphere had changed. It was hushed now, a little sad, just right for late-night confidences.

"I still can't believe she's gone," Sue said quietly, shaking her head and shutting her eyes. "She was so much more alive than other people."

"Her flame burned brighter," said Meredith, gazing at the patterns the rose-and-gold lamp made on the ceiling. Her voice was soft but intense, and it seemed to Bonnie that those words described Elena better than anything she'd ever heard.

"There were times when I hated her, but I could never ignore her," Caroline admitted, her green eyes narrowed in memory. "She wasn't a person you could ignore."

"One thing I learned from her death," Sue said, "is that it could happen to any of us. You can't waste any of life because you never know how long you've got."

"It could be sixty years or sixty minutes," Vickie agreed in a low voice. "Any of us could die tonight."

Bonnie wriggled, disturbed. But before she could say anything, Sue repeated, "I still can't believe she's really gone. Sometimes I feel as if she's somewhere near."

"Oh, so do I," said Bonnie, distracted. An image of Warm Springs flashed through her mind, and for a moment it seemed more vivid than Caroline's dim room. "Last night I dreamed about her, and I had the feeling it really *was* her and that she was trying to tell me something. I still have that feeling," she said to Meredith.

The others gazed at her silently. Once, they would all have laughed if Bonnie hinted at anything supernatural, but not now. Her psychic powers were undisputed, awesome, and a little scary.

"Do you really?" breathed Vickie.

"What do you think she was trying to say?" asked Sue.

"I don't know. At the end she was trying so hard to stay in contact with me, but she couldn't."

There was another silence. At last Sue said hesitantly, with the faintest catch in her voice, "Do you think . . . do you think *you* could contact *her*?"

It was what they'd all been wondering. Bonnie looked toward Meredith. Earlier, Meredith had dismissed the dream, but now she met Bonnie's eyes seriously.

"I don't know," Bonnie said slowly. Visions from the nightmare kept swirling around her. "I don't want to go into a trance and open myself up to whatever else might be out there, that's for sure."

"Is that the only way to communicate with dead people? What about a Ouija board or something?" Sue asked.

"My parents have a Ouija board," Caroline said a little too loudly. Suddenly the hushed, low-key mood was broken and an indefinable tension filled the air. Everyone sat up straighter and looked at each other with speculation. Even Vickie looked intrigued on top of her scaredness.

"Would it work?" Meredith said to Bonnie.

"Should we?" Sue wondered aloud.

"Do we dare? That's really the question," Meredith said. Once again Bonnie found everyone looking at her. She hesitated a final instant, and then shrugged. Excitement was stirring in her stomach.

"Why not?" she said. "What have we got to lose?"

Caroline turned to Vickie. "Vickie, there's a closet at the bottom of the stairs. The Ouija board should be inside, on the top shelf with a bunch of other games."

She didn't even say, "Please, will you get it?" Bonnie frowned and opened her mouth, but Vickie was already out the door.

"You could be a little more gracious," Bonnie

told Caroline. "What is this, your impression of Cinderella's evil stepmother?"

"Oh, come on, Bonnie," Caroline said impatiently. "She's lucky just to be invited. *She* knows that."

"And here I thought she was just overcome by our collective splendor," Meredith said dryly.

"And besides—" Bonnie started when she was interrupted. The noise was thin and shrill and it fell off weakly at the end, but there was no mistaking it. It was a scream. It was followed by dead silence and then suddenly peal after peal of piercing shrieks.

For an instant the girls in the bedroom stood transfixed. Then they were all running out into the hallway and down the stairs.

"Vickie!" Meredith, with her long legs, reached the bottom first. Vickie was standing in front of the closet, arms outstretched as if to protect her face. She clutched at Meredith, still screaming.

"Vickie, what is it?" Caroline demanded, sounding more angry than afraid. There were game boxes scattered across the floor and Monopoly markers and Trivial Pursuit cards strewn everywhere. "What are you yelling about?"

"It grabbed me! I was reaching up to the top shelf and something grabbed me around the waist!"

"From behind?"

"No! From inside the closet."

Startled, Bonnie looked inside the open closet. Winter coats hung in an impenetrable layer, some of them reaching the floor. Gently disengaging herself from Vickie, Meredith picked up an umbrella and began poking the coats.

"Oh, don't—" Bonnie began involuntarily, but the umbrella encountered only the resistance of cloth. Meredith used it to push the coats aside and reveal the bare cedarwood of the closet wall.

"You see? Nobody there," she said lightly. "But you know what *is* there are these coat sleeves. If you leaned in far enough between them, I'll bet it could feel like somebody's arms closing around you."

Vickie stepped forward, touched a dangling sleeve, then looked up at the shelf. She put her face in her hands, long silky hair falling forward to screen it. For an awful moment Bonnie thought she was crying, then she heard the giggles.

"Oh, God! I really thought—oh, I'm so stupid! I'll clean it up," Vickie said.

"Later," said Meredith firmly. "Let's go in the living room."

Bonnie threw one last look at the closet as they went.

When they were all gathered around the coffee table, with several lights turned off for effect, Bonnie put her fingers lightly on the small plastic planchette. She'd never actually used a Ouija board, but she knew how it was done. The planchette moved to point at letters and spell out a message—if the spirits were willing to talk, that is.

"We all have to be touching it," she said, and then watched as the others obeyed. Meredith's fingers were long and slender, Sue's slim and tapering with oval nails. Caroline's nails were painted burnished copper. Vickie's were bitten.

"Now we close our eyes and concentrate," Bonnie said softly. There were little hisses of anticipation as the girls obeyed; the atmosphere was getting to all of them.

"Think of Elena. Picture her. If she's out there, we want to draw her here."

The big room was silent. In the dark behind her closed lids Bonnie saw pale gold hair and eyes like lapis lazuli.

"Come on, Elena," she whispered. "Talk to me."

The planchette began to move.

None of them could be guiding it; they were all applying pressure from different points. Nevertheless, the little triangle of plastic was sliding smoothly, confidently. Bonnie kept her eyes shut until it stopped and then looked. The planchette was pointing to the word *Yes*.

Vickie gave something like a soft sob.

Bonnie looked at the others. Caroline was breathing fast, green eyes narrowed. Sue, the only one of all of them, still had her eyes resolutely closed. Meredith looked pale.

They all expected her to know what to do.

"Keep concentrating," Bonnie told them. She felt unready and a little stupid addressing the empty air directly. But she was the expert; she had to do it.

"Is that you, Elena?" she said.

The planchette made a little circle and returned to *Yes*.

Suddenly Bonnie's heart was beating so hard she was afraid it would shake her fingers. The plastic underneath her fingertips felt different, electrified almost, as if some supernatural energy was flowing through it. She no longer felt stupid. Tears came to her eyes, and she could see that Meredith's eyes were glistening too. Meredith nodded at her.

"How can we be sure?" Caroline was saying, loudly, suspiciously. Caroline doesn't feel it, Bonnie realized; she doesn't sense anything I do. Psychically speaking, she's a dud.

The planchette was moving again, touching letters now, so quickly that Meredith barely had time to spell out the message. Even without punctuation it was clear.

CAROLINE DONT BE A JERK, it said. YOURE LUCKY IM TALKING TO YOU AT ALL

"That's Elena, all right," Meredith said dryly.

"It sounds like her, but—"

"Oh, shut up, Caroline," Bonnie said. "Elena, I'm just so glad . . ." Her throat locked up and she tried again.

BONNIE THERES NO TIME   STOP SNIVELING AND GET DOWN TO BUSINESS

And *that* was Elena too. Bonnie sniffed and went on. "I had a dream about you last night."

TEA

"Yes." Bonnie's heart was thudding faster than ever. "I wanted to talk to you, but things got weird and then we kept losing contact—"

BONNIE DONT TRANCE   NO TRANCE   NO TRANCE

"All right." That answered her question, and she was relieved to hear it.

CORRUPTING INFLUENCES DISTORTING OUR COMMUNICATION   THERE ARE BAD THINGS VERY BAD THINGS OUT HERE

"Like what?" Bonnie leaned closer to the board. "Like what?"

NO TIME! The planchette seemed to add the exclamation point. It was jerking violently from letter to letter as if Elena could barely contain her impatience. HES BUSY SO I CAN TALK NOW BUT

THERES NOT MUCH TIME LISTEN WHEN WE STOP GET OUT OF THE HOUSE FAST YOURE IN DANGER

"Danger?" Vickie repeated, looking as if she might jump off the chair and run.

WAIT LISTEN FIRST THE WHOLE TOWN IS IN DANGER

"What do we do?" said Meredith instantly.

YOU NEED HELP HES OUT OF YOUR LEAGUE UNBELIEVABLY STRONG NOW LISTEN AND FOLLOW INSTRUCTIONS YOU HAVE TO DO A SUMMONING SPELL AND THE FIRST INGREDIENT IS H—

Without warning, the planchette jerked away from the letters and flew around the board wildly. It pointed at the stylized picture of the moon, then at the sun, then at the words *Parker Brothers, Inc.*

"Elena!"

The planchette bobbed back to the letters.

ANOTHER MOUSE ANOTHER MOUSE ANOTHER MOUSE

"What's happening?" Sue cried, eyes wide open now.

Bonnie was frightened. The planchette was pulsing with energy, a dark and ugly energy like boiling black tar that stung her fingers. But she could also feel the quivering silver thread that was Elena's presence fighting it. "Don't let go!" she cried desperately. "Don't take your hands off it!"

MOUSEMUDKILLYOU, the board reeled off. BLOOD-

BLOODBLOOD. And then . . . BONNIE GET OUT RUN HES HERE RUN RUN RU—

The planchette jerked furiously, whipping out from under Bonnie's fingers and beyond her reach, flying across the board and through the air as if someone had thrown it. Vickie screamed. Meredith started to her feet.

And then all the lights went out, plunging the house into darkness.

Three

Vickie's screams went out of control. Bonnie could feel panic rising in her chest.

"Vickie, stop it! Come on; we've got to get out of here!" Meredith was shouting to be heard. "It's your house, Caroline. Everybody grab hands and you lead us to the front door."

"Okay," Caroline said. She didn't sound as frightened as everybody else. That was the advantage to having no imagination, Bonnie thought. You couldn't picture the terrible things that were going to happen to you.

She felt better with Meredith's narrow, cold hand grasping hers. She fumbled on the other side and caught Caroline's, feeling the hardness of long fingernails.

She could see nothing. Her eyes should be adjusting to the dark by now, but she couldn't make out even a glimmer of light or shadow as Caroline started leading them. There was no light coming through the windows from the street; the power seemed to be out everywhere. Caroline cursed, running into some piece of furniture, and Bonnie stumbled against her.

Vickie was whimpering softly from the back of the line. "Hang on," whispered Sue. "Hang on, Vickie, we'll make it."

They made slow, shuffling progress in the dark. Then Bonnie felt tile under her feet. "This is the front hall," Caroline said. "Stay here a minute while I find the door." Her fingers slipped out of Bonnie's.

"Caroline! Don't let go—where are you? Caroline, give me your hand!" Bonnie cried, groping frantically like a blind person.

Out of the darkness something large and moist closed around her fingers. It was a hand. It wasn't Caroline's.

Bonnie screamed.

Vickie immediately picked it up, shrieking wildly. The hot, moist hand was dragging Bonnie forward. She kicked out, struggling, but it made no difference. Then she felt Meredith's arms around her waist, both arms, wrenching her back. Her hand came free of the big one.

And then she was turning and running, just running, only dimly aware that Meredith was beside her. She wasn't at all aware that she was still screaming until she slammed into a large armchair that stopped her progress, and she heard herself.

"Hush! Bonnie, hush, stop!" Meredith was shaking her. They had slid down the back of the chair to the floor.

"Something had me! Something grabbed me, Meredith!"

"I know. Be quiet! It's still around," Meredith said. Bonnie jammed her face into Meredith's shoulder to keep from screaming again. What if it was here in the room with them?

Seconds crawled past, and the silence pooled around them. No matter how Bonnie strained her ears, she could hear no sound except their own breathing and the dull thudding of her heart.

"Listen! We've got to find the back door. We must be in the living room now. That means the kitchen's right behind us. We have to get there," Meredith said, her voice low.

Bonnie started to nod miserably, then abruptly lifted her head. "Where's Vickie?" she whispered hoarsely.

"I don't know. I had to let go of her hand to pull you away from that thing. Let's move."

Bonnie held her back. "But why isn't she screaming?"

A shudder went through Meredith. "I don't know."

"Oh, God. Oh, God. We can't leave her, Meredith."

"We *have* to."

"We *can't*. Meredith, I made Caroline invite her. She wouldn't be here except for me. We have to get her out."

There was a pause, and then Meredith hissed, "All right! But you pick the strangest times to turn noble, Bonnie."

A door slammed, causing both of them to jump. Then there was a crashing, like feet on stairs, Bonnie thought. And briefly, a voice was raised.

"Vickie, where are you? Don't—Vickie, no! No!"

"That was Sue," gasped Bonnie, jumping up. "From upstairs!"

"Why don't we have a *flashlight*?" Meredith was raging.

Bonnie knew what she meant. It was too dark to go running blindly around this house; it was too frightening. There was a primitive panic hammering in her brain. She needed light, any light.

She couldn't go fumbling into that darkness again, exposed on all sides. She couldn't *do* it.

Nevertheless, she took one shaky step away from the chair.

"Come on," she gasped, and Meredith came with her, step by step, into the blackness.

Bonnie kept expecting that moist, hot hand to reach out and grab her again. Every inch of her skin tingled in anticipation of its touch, and especially her own hand, which she had outstretched to feel her way.

Then she made the mistake of remembering the dream.

Instantly, the sickly sweet smell of garbage overwhelmed her. She imagined things crawling out of the ground and then remembered Elena's face, gray and hairless, with lips shriveled back from grinning teeth. If *that thing* grabbed hold of her . . .

I can't go any farther; I can't, I can't, she thought. I'm sorry for Vickie, but I can't go on. Please, just let me stop here.

She was clinging to Meredith, almost crying. Then from upstairs came the most horrifying sound she had ever heard.

It was a whole series of sounds, actually, but they all came so close together that they blended into one terrible swell of noise. First there was screaming, Sue's voice screaming, "Vickie! Vickie! No!" Then a resonant crash, the sound of glass shattering, as if a hundred windows were breaking at once. And over that a sustained scream, on a note of pure, exquisite terror.

Then it all stopped.

"*What was it?* What happened, Meredith?"

"Something bad." Meredith's voice was taut and choked. "Something very bad. Bonnie, let go. I'm going to see."

"Not alone, you're not," Bonnie said fiercely.

They found the staircase and made their way up it. When they reached the landing, Bonnie could hear a strange and oddly sickening sound, the tinkle of glass shards falling.

And then the lights went on.

It was too sudden; Bonnie screamed involuntarily. Turning to Meredith she almost screamed again. Meredith's dark hair was disheveled and her cheekbones looked too sharp; her face was pale and hollow with fear.

Tinkle, tinkle.

It was *worse* with the lights on. Meredith was walking toward the last door down the hall, where the noise was coming from. Bonnie followed, but she knew suddenly, with all her heart, that she didn't want to see inside that room.

Meredith pulled the door open. She froze for a minute in the doorway and then lunged quickly inside. Bonnie started for the door.

"Oh, my God, don't come any farther!"

Bonnie didn't even pause. She plunged into

the doorway and then pulled up short. At first glance it looked as if the whole side of the house was gone. The French windows that connected the master bedroom to the balcony seemed to have exploded outward, the wood splintered, the glass shattered. Little pieces of glass were hanging precariously here and there from the remnants of the wood frame. They tinkled as they fell.

Diaphanous white curtains billowed in and out of the gaping hole in the house. In front of them, in silhouette, Bonnie could see Vickie. She was standing with her hands at her sides, as motionless as a block of stone.

"Vickie, are you okay?" Bonnie was so relieved to see her alive that it was painful. "Vickie?"

Vickie didn't turn, didn't answer. Bonnie maneuvered around her cautiously, looking into her face. Vickie was staring straight ahead, her pupils pinpoints. She was sucking in little whistling breaths, chest heaving.

"I'm next. It said I'm next," she whispered over and over, but she didn't seem to be talking to Bonnie. She didn't seem to see Bonnie at all.

Shuddering, Bonnie reeled away. Meredith was on the balcony. She turned as Bonnie reached the curtains and tried to block the way.

"Don't look. Don't look down there," she said.

Down *where*? Suddenly Bonnie understood. She shoved past Meredith, who caught her arm to stop her on the edge of a dizzying drop. The balcony railing had been blasted out like the French windows and Bonnie could see straight down to the lighted yard below. On the ground there was a twisted figure like a broken doll, limbs askew, neck bent at a grotesque angle, blond hair fanned on the dark soil of the garden. It was Sue Carson.

And throughout all the confusion that raged afterward, two thoughts kept vying for dominance in Bonnie's mind. One was that Caroline would never have her foursome now. And the other was that it wasn't fair for this to happen on Meredith's birthday. It just wasn't fair.

"I'm sorry, Meredith. I don't think she's up to it right now."

Bonnie heard her father's voice at the front door as she listlessly stirred sweetener into a cup of chamomile tea. She put the spoon down at once. What she wasn't up to was sitting in this kitchen one minute longer. She needed out.

"I'll be right there, Dad."

Meredith looked almost as bad as she had last

night, face peaked, eyes shadowed. Her mouth was set in a tight line.

"We'll just go out driving for a little while," Bonnie said to her father. "Maybe see some of the kids. After all, you're the one who said it isn't dangerous, right?"

What could he say? Mr. McCullough looked down at his petite daughter, who stuck out the stubborn chin she'd inherited from him and met his gaze squarely. He lifted his hands.

"It's almost four o'clock now. Be back before dark," he said.

"They want it both ways," Bonnie said to Meredith on the way to Meredith's car. Once inside, both girls immediately locked their doors.

As Meredith put the car in gear she gave Bonnie a glance of grim understanding.

"Your parents didn't believe you, either."

"Oh, they believe everything I told them—except anything important. How can they be so *stupid*?"

Meredith laughed shortly. "You've got to look at it from their point of view. They find one dead body without a mark on it except those caused by the fall. They find that the lights were off in the neighborhood because of a malfunction at Virginia Electric. They find us, hysterical, giving answers to their questions that must have seemed pretty weird. Who did it? Some monster with sweaty hands. How do we know? Our dead friend Elena told us through a Ouija board. Is it any wonder they have their doubts?"

"If they'd never seen anything like it *before*," Bonnie said, hitting the car door with her fist. "But they *have*. Do they think we made up those dogs that attacked at the Snow Dance last year? Do they think Elena was killed by a fantasy?"

"They're forgetting already," Meredith replied softly. "You predicted it yourself. Life has gone back to normal, and everybody in Fell's Church feels safer that way. They all feel like they've woken up from a bad dream, and the last thing they want is to get sucked in again."

Bonnie just shook her head.

"And so it's easier to believe that a bunch of teenage girls got riled up playing with a Ouija board, and that when the lights went out they just freaked and ran. And one of them got so scared and confused she ran right out a window."

There was a silence and then Meredith added, "I wish Alaric were here."

Normally, Bonnie would have given her a dig in the ribs and answered, "So do *I*," in a lecherous voice. Alaric was one of the handsomest guys she'd ever seen, even if he was a doddering twenty-two years old. Now, she just gave Meredith's arm a disconsolate squeeze. "Can't you call him somehow?"

"In Russia? I don't even know *where* in Russia he is now."

Bonnie bit her lip.

Then she sat up. Meredith was driving down Lee Street, and in the high school parking lot they could see a crowd.

She and Meredith exchanged glances, and Meredith nodded. "We might as well," she said. "Let's see if they're any smarter than their parents."

Bonnie could see startled faces turning as the car cruised slowly into the lot. When she and Meredith got out, people moved back, making a path for them to the center of the crowd.

Caroline was there, clutching her elbows with her hands and shaking back her auburn hair distractedly.

"We're not going to sleep in that house again until it's repaired," she was saying, shivering in her white sweater. "Daddy says we'll take an apartment in Heron until it's over."

"What difference does that make? He can follow you to Heron, I'm sure," said Meredith.

Caroline turned, but her green cat's eyes wouldn't quite meet Meredith's. "Who?" she said vaguely.

"Oh, Caroline, not you too!" Bonnie exploded.

"I just want to get out of here," Caroline said.

Her eyes came up and for an instant Bonnie saw how frightened she was. "I can't take any more." As if she had to prove her words that minute, she pushed her way through the crowd.

"Let her go, Bonnie," Meredith said. "It's no use."

"*She's* no use," said Bonnie furiously. If Caroline, who *knew*, was acting this way, what about the other kids?

She saw the answer in the faces around her. Everybody looked scared, as scared as if she and Meredith had brought some loathsome disease with them. As if she and Meredith were the problem.

"I don't believe this," Bonnie muttered.

"I don't believe it either," said Deanna Kennedy, a friend of Sue's. She was in the front of the crowd, and she didn't look as uneasy as the others. "I talked with Sue yesterday afternoon and she was so up, so happy. She *can't* be dead." Deanna began to sob. Her boyfriend put an arm around her, and several other girls began to cry. The guys in the crowd shifted, their faces rigid.

Bonnie felt a little surge of hope. "And she's not going to be the only one dead," she added. "Elena told us that the whole town is in danger. Elena said . . ." Despite herself Bonnie heard her voice failing. She could see it in the way their eyes glazed up when she mentioned Elena's name. Meredith was right; they'd put everything that had happened last winter behind them. They didn't believe anymore.

"What's *wrong* with you all?" she said helplessly, wanting to hit something. "You don't really think Sue threw herself off that balcony!"

"People are saying—" Deanna's boyfriend started and then shrugged defensively. "Well—you told the police Vickie Bennett was in the room, right? And now she's off her head again. And just a little bit earlier you'd heard Sue shouting, 'No, Vickie, no!'?"

Bonnie felt as if the wind had been knocked out of her. "You think that *Vickie*—oh, God, you're out of your mind! Listen to me. Something grabbed my hand in that house, and it *wasn't* Vickie. And Vickie had nothing to do with throwing Sue off that balcony."

"She's hardly strong enough, for one thing," Meredith said pointedly. "She weighs about ninety-five pounds soaking wet."

Somebody from the back of the crowd muttered about insane people having superhuman strength. "Vickie has a psychiatric record—"

"Elena told us it was a guy!" Bonnie almost shouted, losing her battle with self-control. The faces tilted toward her were shuttered, unyielding. Then she saw one that made her chest loosen. "Matt! Tell them you believe us."

Matt Honeycutt was standing on the fringe with his hands in his pockets and his blond head bowed. Now he looked up, and what Bonnie saw in his blue eyes made her draw in her breath. They weren't hard and shuttered like everyone else's, but they were full of a flat despair that was just as bad. He shrugged without taking his hands from his pockets.

"For what it's worth, I believe you," he said. "But what difference does it make? It's all going to turn out the same anyway."

Bonnie, for one of the first times in her life, was speechless. Matt had been upset ever since Elena died, but this . . .

"He does believe it, though," Meredith was saying quickly, capitalizing on the moment. "Now what have we got to do to convince the rest of you?"

"Channel Elvis for us, maybe," said a voice that immediately set Bonnie's blood boiling. Tyler. Tyler Smallwood. Grinning like an ape in his overexpensive Perry Ellis sweater, showing a mouthful of strong white teeth.

"It's not as good as psychic e-mail from a dead Homecoming Queen, but it's a start," Tyler added.

Matt always said that grin was asking for a punch in the nose. But Matt, the only guy in the crowd with close to Tyler's physique, was staring dully at the ground.

"Shut up, Tyler! You don't know what happened in that house," Bonnie said.

"Well, neither do you, apparently. Maybe if you hadn't been hiding in the living room, you'd have seen what happened. Then somebody might believe you."

Bonnie's retort died on her tongue. She stared at Tyler, opened her mouth, and then closed it. Tyler waited. When she didn't speak, he showed his teeth again.

"For my money, Vickie did it," he said, winking at Dick Carter, Vickie's ex-boyfriend. "She's a strong little babe, right, Dick? She *could* have done it." He turned and added deliberately over his shoulder, "Or else that Salvatore guy is back in town."

"You creep!" shouted Bonnie. Even Meredith cried out in frustration. Because of course at the very mention of Stefan pandemonium ensued, as Tyler must have known it would. Everyone was turning to the person next to them and exclaiming in alarm, horror, excitement. It was primarily the girls who were excited.

Effectively, it put an end to the gathering. People had been edging away surreptitiously before, and now they broke up into twos and threes, arguing and hastening off.

Bonnie gazed after them angrily.

"Supposing they did believe you. What did you want them to do, anyway?" Matt said. She hadn't noticed him beside her.

"I don't know. Something besides just standing around waiting to be picked off." She tried to look him in the face. "Matt, are you all right?"

"I don't know. Are you?"

Bonnie thought. "No. I mean, in one way I'm surprised I'm doing as well as I am, because when Elena died, I just couldn't deal. At all. But then I wasn't as close to Sue, and besides . . . I don't know!" She wanted to hit something again. "It's just all too much!"

"You're mad."

"*Yes*, I'm mad." Suddenly Bonnie understood the feelings she'd been having all day. "Killing Sue wasn't just wrong, it was *evil*. Truly evil. And whoever did it isn't going to get away with it. That would be—if the world is like that, a place where that can happen and go unpunished . . . if that's the truth . . ." She found she didn't have a way to finish.

"Then what? You don't want to live here anymore? What if the world *is* like that?"

His eyes were so lost, so bitter. Bonnie was shaken. But she said staunchly, "I won't *let* it be that way. And you won't either."

He simply looked at her as if she were a kid insisting there was so a Santa Claus.

Meredith spoke up. "If we expect other people to take us seriously, we'd better take ourselves seriously. Elena *did* communicate with us. She wanted us to do something. Now if we really believe that, we'd better figure out what it is."

Matt's face had flexed at the mention of Elena. You poor guy, you're still as much in love with her as ever, thought Bonnie. I wonder if anything could make you forget her? She said, "Are you going to help us, Matt?"

"I'll help," Matt said quietly. "But I still don't know what it is you're doing."

"We're going to stop that murdering creep before he kills anybody else," said Bonnie. It was the first time she'd fully realized herself that this was what she meant to do.

"Alone? Because you are alone, you know."

"*We* are alone," Meredith corrected. "But that's what Elena was trying to tell us. She said we had to do a summoning spell to call for help."

"An easy spell with only two ingredients," Bonnie remembered from her dream. She was getting excited. "And she said she'd already told me the ingredients—but she hadn't."

"Last night she said there were corrupting influences distorting her communication," Meredith said. "Now to me that sounds like what was happening in the dream. Do you think it really *was* Elena you were drinking tea with?"

"Yes," Bonnie said positively. "I mean, I know we weren't really having a mad tea party at Warm Springs, but I think Elena was sending that message into my brain. And then partway through something else took over and pushed her out. But she fought, and for a minute at the end she got back control."

"Okay. Then that means we have to concentrate on the beginning of the dream, when it was still Elena communicating with you. But if what she was saying was already being distorted by other influences, then maybe it came out weird. Maybe it wasn't something she actually said, maybe it was something she did . . ."

Bonnie's hand flew up to touch her curls. "Hair!" she cried.

"What?"

"Hair! I asked her who did hers, and we talked about it, and she said, 'Hair is very important.' And Meredith—when she was trying to tell us the ingredients last night, the first letter of one of them was *H*!"

"That's it!" Meredith's dark eyes were flashing. "Now we just have to think of the other one."

"But I know that too!" Bonnie's laughter bubbled up exuberantly. "She told me right after we talked about hair, and I thought she was just being strange. She said, 'Blood is important too.' "

Meredith shut her eyes in realization. "And last night, the Ouija board said 'Bloodblood-blood.' I thought it was the other thing threatening us, but it wasn't," she said. She opened her eyes. "Bonnie, do you think that's really it? Are those the ingredients, or do we have to start worrying about mud and sandwiches and mice and tea?"

"Those are the ingredients," Bonnie said firmly. "They're the kind of ingredients that make sense for a summoning spell. I'm sure I can find a ritual to do with them in one of my Celtic magic books. We just have to figure out the person we're supposed to summon . . ." Something struck her, and her voice trailed off in dismay.

"I was wondering when you'd notice," Matt said, speaking for the first time in a long while. "You don't know who it is, do you?"

Four

Meredith tilted an ironic glance at Matt. "Hmm," she said. "Now, who do you *think* Elena would call in time of trouble?"

Bonnie's grin gave way to a twinge of guilt at Matt's expression. It wasn't fair to tease him about this. "Elena said that the killer is too strong for us and that's why we need help," she told Matt. "And I can think of only one person Elena knows who could fight off a psychic killer."

Slowly, Matt nodded. Bonnie couldn't tell what he was feeling. He and Stefan had been best friends once, even after Elena had chosen Stefan over Matt. But that had been before Matt found out what Stefan was, and what kind of violence he was capable of. In his rage and grief over Elena's death Stefan had nearly killed Tyler

Smallwood and five other guys. Could Matt really forget that? Could he even deal with Stefan coming back to Fell's Church?

Matt's square-jawed face gave no sign now, and Meredith was talking again. "So all we need to do is let some blood and cut some hair. You won't miss a curl or two, will you, Bonnie?"

Bonnie was so abstracted that she almost missed this. Then she shook her head. "No, no, no. It isn't *our* blood and hair we need. We need it from the person we want to summon."

"What? But that's ridiculous. If we had *Stefan's* blood and hair we wouldn't *need* to summon him, would we?"

"I didn't think of that," Bonnie admitted. "Usually with a summoning spell you get the stuff beforehand and use it when you want to call a person back. What are we going to do, Meredith? It's impossible."

Meredith's brows were drawn together. "Why would Elena ask it if it were impossible?"

"Elena asked lots of impossible things," Bonnie said darkly. "Don't look like that, Matt; you know she did. She wasn't a saint."

"Maybe, but this one isn't impossible," Matt said. "I can think of one place where Stefan's blood has got to be, and if we're lucky some of his hair, too. In the crypt."

Bonnie flinched, but Meredith simply nodded.

"Of course," she said. "While Stefan was tied up there, he must have bled all over the place. And in that kind of fight he might have lost some hair. If only everything down there has been left undisturbed . . ."

"I don't think anybody's been down there since Elena died," Matt said. "The police investigated and then left it. But there's only one way to find out."

I was wrong, Bonnie thought. I was worrying about whether Matt could deal with Stefan coming back, and here he is doing everything he can to help us summon him. "Matt, I could kiss you!" she said.

For an instant something she couldn't identify flickered in Matt's eyes. Surprise, certainly, but there was more than that. Suddenly Bonnie wondered what he would do if she *did* kiss him.

"All the girls say that," he replied calmly at last, with a shrug of mock resignation. It was as close as he'd gotten to lightheartedness all day.

Meredith, however, was serious. "Let's go. We've got a lot to do, and the last thing we want is to get stuck in the crypt after dark."

The crypt was beneath the ruined church that stood on a hill in the cemetery. It's only late afternoon, plenty of light left, Bonnie kept telling herself as they walked up the hill, but gooseflesh broke out on her arms anyway. The modern cemetery on one side was bad enough, but the old graveyard on the other side was downright spooky even in daylight. There were so many crumbling headstones tilting crazily in the overgrown grass, representing so many young men killed in the Civil War. You didn't have to be psychic to feel their presence.

"Unquiet spirits," she muttered.

"Hmm?" said Meredith as she stepped over the pile of rubble that was one wall of the ruined church. "Look, the lid of the tomb's still off. That's good news; I don't think we would have been able to lift it."

Bonnie's eyes lingered wistfully on the white marble statues carved on the displaced lid. Honoria Fell lay there with her husband, hands folded on her breast, looking as gentle and sad as ever. But Bonnie knew there would be no more help from that quarter. Honoria's duties as protector of the town she'd founded were done.

Leaving Elena holding the bag, Bonnie thought grimly, looking down into the rectangular hole that led to the crypt. Iron rungs disappeared into darkness.

Even with the help of Meredith's flashlight it was hard to climb down into that underground room. Inside, it was dank and silent, the walls faced with polished stone. Bonnie tried not to shiver.

"Look," said Meredith quietly.

Matt had the flashlight trained on the iron gate that separated the anteroom of the crypt from its main chamber. The stone below was stained black with blood in several places. Looking at the puddles and rivulets of dried gore made Bonnie feel dizzy.

"We know Damon was hurt the worst," Meredith said, moving forward. She sounded calm, but Bonnie could hear the tight control in her voice. "So he must have been on this side where there's the most blood. Stefan said Elena was in the center. That means Stefan himself must have been . . . here." She bent down.

"I'll do it," Matt said gruffly. "You hold the light." With a plastic picnic knife from Meredith's car he scraped at the encrusted stone. Bonnie swallowed, glad she'd had only tea for lunch. Blood was all right in the abstract, but when you were actually confronted with so much of it—especially when it was the blood of a friend who'd been tortured . . .

Bonnie turned away, looking at the stone walls and thinking about Katherine. Both Stefan and his older brother, Damon, had been in love with Katherine, back in fifteenth-century Florence. But what they hadn't known was that the girl they loved wasn't human. A vampire in her own German village had changed her to save her life when she was ill. Katherine in her turn had made both the boys vampires.

And then, thought Bonnie, she faked her own death to get Stefan and Damon to stop fighting over her. But it didn't work. They hated each other more than ever, and she hated both of them for *that*. She'd gone back to the vampire who made her, and over the years she'd turned as evil as he was. Until at last all she wanted to do was destroy the brothers she had once loved. She'd lured them both to Fell's Church to kill them, and this room was where she'd almost succeeded in doing it. Elena had died stopping her.

"There," Matt said, and Bonnie blinked and came back to herself. Matt was standing with a paper napkin that now held flakes of Stefan's blood in its folds. "Now the hair," he said.

They swept the floor with their fingers, finding dust and bits of leaves and fragments of things Bonnie didn't want to identify. Among the detritus were long strands of pale gold hair. Elena's —or Katherine's, Bonnie thought. They had looked much alike. There were also shorter strands of dark hair, crisp with a slight wave. Stefan's.

It was slow, finicky work sorting through it all and putting the right hairs in another napkin.

Matt did most of it. When they were through, they were all tired and the light sifting down through the rectangular opening in the ceiling was dim blue. But Meredith smiled tigerishly.

"We've got it," she said. "Tyler wants Stefan back; well, we'll *give* him Stefan back."

And Bonnie, who had been only half paying attention to what she was doing, still lost in her own thoughts, froze.

She'd been thinking about other things entirely, nothing to do with Tyler, but at the mention of his name something had winked on in her mind. Something she'd realized in the parking lot and then forgotten afterward in the heat of arguing. Meredith's words had triggered it and now it was suddenly all clear again. How had he *known*? she wondered, heart racing.

"Bonnie? What's the matter?"

"Meredith," she said softly, "did you tell the police specifically that we were in the living room when everything was going on upstairs with Sue?"

"No, I think I just said we were downstairs. Why?"

"Because I didn't either. And Vickie couldn't have told them because she's gone catatonic again, and Sue's dead and Caroline was outside by that time. *But Tyler knew*. Remember, he said, 'If you hadn't been hiding in the living room, you'd have seen what happened.' How could he know?"

"Bonnie, if you're trying to suggest Tyler was the murderer, it just won't wash. He's not smart enough to organize a killing spree, for one thing," Meredith said.

"But there's something else. Meredith, last year at the Junior Prom, Tyler touched me on my bare shoulder. I'll never forget it. His hand was big, and meaty, and hot, and damp." Bonnie shivered at the recollection. "Just like the hand that grabbed me last night."

But Meredith was shaking her head, and even Matt looked unconvinced.

"Elena's sure wasting her time asking us to bring back Stefan, then," he said. "I could take care of Tyler with a couple of right hooks."

"Think about it, Bonnie," Meredith added. "Does Tyler have the psychic power to move a Ouija board or come into your dreams? *Does he?*"

He didn't. Psychically speaking, Tyler was as much a dud as Caroline. Bonnie couldn't deny it. But she couldn't deny her intuition, either. It didn't make sense, but she still felt Tyler had been in the house last night.

"We'd better get moving," Meredith said. "It's dark, and your father's going to be furious."

They were all silent on the ride home. Bonnie

was still thinking about Tyler. Once at her house they smuggled the napkins upstairs and began looking through Bonnie's books on Druids and Celtic magic. Ever since she'd discovered that she was descended from the ancient race of magic workers, Bonnie had been interested in the Druids. And in one of the books she found a ritual for a summoning spell.

"We need to buy candles," she said. "And pure water—better get some bottled," she said to Meredith. "And chalk to draw a circle on the floor, and something to make a small fire in. I can find those in the house. There's no hurry; the spell has to be done at midnight."

Midnight was a long time coming. Meredith bought the necessary items at a grocery store and brought them back. They ate dinner with Bonnie's family, though no one had much of an appetite. By eleven o'clock Bonnie had the circle drawn on the hardwood floor of her bedroom and all the other ingredients on a low bench inside the circle. On the stroke of twelve she started.

With Matt and Meredith watching, she made a small fire in an earthenware bowl. Three candles were burning behind the bowl; she stuck a pin halfway down the one in the center. Then she unfolded a napkin and carefully stirred the dried flakes of blood into a wineglass of water. It turned rusty pink.

She opened the other napkin. Three pinches of dark hair went into the fire, sizzling with a terrible smell. Then three drops of the stained water, hissing.

Her eyes went to the words in the open book.

Swift on the heel thou comest,
Thrice summoned by my spell,
Thrice troubled by my burning.
Come to me without delay.

She read the words aloud slowly, three times. Then she sat back on her heels. The fire went on burning smokily. The candle flames danced.

"And now what?" Matt said.

"I don't know. It just says wait for the middle candle to burn down to the pin."

"And what then?"

"I guess we'll find out when it happens."

In Florence, it was dawn.

Stefan watched the girl move down the stairway, one hand resting lightly on the banister to keep her balance. Her movements were slow and slightly dreamlike, as if she were floating.

Suddenly, she swayed and clutched at the banister more tightly. Stefan moved quickly behind her and put a hand under her elbow.

"Are you all right?"

She looked up at him with the same dreaminess. She was very pretty. Her expensive clothes were the latest fashion and her stylishly disarrayed hair was blond. A tourist. He knew she was American before she spoke.

"Yes . . . I think . . ." Her brown eyes were unfocused.

"Do you have a way to get home? Where are you staying?"

"On Via dei Conti, near the Medici chapel. I'm with the Gonzaga in Florence program."

Damn! Not a tourist, then; a student. And that meant she'd be carrying this story back with her, telling her classmates about the handsome Italian guy she'd met last night. The one with night-dark eyes. The one who took her back to his exclusive place on Via Tornabuoni and wined her and dined her and then, in the moonlight, maybe, in his room or out in the enclosed courtyard, leaned close to look into her eyes and . . .

Stefan's gaze slid away from the girl's throat with its two reddened puncture wounds. He'd seen marks like that so often—how could they still have the power to disturb him? But they did; they sickened him and set a slow burning in his gut.

"What's your name?"

"Rachael. With an *a*." She spelled it.

"All right, Rachael. Look at me. You will go back to your *pensione* and you won't remember anything about last night. You don't know where you went or who you saw. And you've never seen *me* before, either. Repeat."

"I don't remember anything about last night," she said obediently, her eyes on his. Stefan's Powers were not as strong as they would have been if he'd been drinking human blood, but they were strong enough for this. "I don't know where I went or who I saw. I haven't seen you."

"Good. Do you have money to get back? Here." Stefan pulled a fistful of crumpled lire—mostly 50,000 and 100,000 notes—out of his pocket and led her outside.

When she was safely in a cab, he went back inside and made straight for Damon's bedroom.

Damon was lounging near the window, peeling an orange, not even dressed yet. He looked up, annoyed, as Stefan entered.

"It's customary to knock," he said.

"Where'd you meet her?" said Stefan. And then, when Damon turned a blank stare on him, he added, "That girl. Rachael."

"Was that her name? I don't think I bothered to ask. At Bar Gilli. Or perhaps it was Bar Mario. Why?"

Stefan struggled to contain his anger. "That's

not the only thing you didn't bother to do. You didn't bother to influence her to forget you, either. Do you *want* to get caught, Damon?"

Damon's lips curved in a smile and he twisted off a curlicue of orange peel. "I am *never* caught, little brother," he said.

"So what are you going to do when they come after you? When somebody realizes, 'My God, there's a bloodsucking monster on Via Tornabuoni'? Kill them all? Wait until they break down the front door and then melt away into darkness?"

Damon met his gaze directly, challengingly, that faint smile still clinging about his lips.

"Why not?" he said.

"*Damn* you!" said Stefan. "Listen to me, Damon. This has got to stop."

"I'm touched at your concern for my safety."

"It isn't fair, Damon. To take an unwilling girl like that—"

"Oh, she was willing, brother. She was very, very willing."

"Did you tell her what you were going to do? Did you warn her about the consequences of exchanging blood with a vampire? The nightmares, the psychic visions? Was she willing for *that*?" Damon clearly wasn't going to reply, so he went on. "You know it's wrong."

"As a matter of fact, I do." With that, Damon

gave one of his sudden, unnerving smiles, turning it on and off instantly.

"And you don't care," Stefan said dully, looking away.

Damon tossed away the orange. His tone was silky, persuasive. "Little brother, the world is full of what you call 'wrong,' " he said. "Why not relax and join the winning side? It's much more fun, I assure you."

Stefan felt himself go hot with anger. "How can you even say that?" he flashed back. "Didn't you learn anything from Katherine? *She* chose 'the winning side.' "

"Katherine died too quickly," said Damon. He was smiling again, but his eyes were cold.

"And now all you can think about is revenge." Looking at his brother, Stefan felt a crushing weight settle on his own chest. "That and your own pleasure," he said.

"What else is there? Pleasure is the only reality, little brother—pleasure and power. And you're a hunter by nature, just as much as I am," Damon said. He added, "I don't remember inviting you to come to Florence with me, anyway. Since you're not enjoying yourself, why don't you just leave?"

The weight in Stefan's chest tightened suddenly, unbearably, but his gaze, locked with Damon's, did not waver. "You know why," he said quietly. And at last he had the satisfaction of seeing Damon's eyes drop.

Stefan himself could hear Elena's words in his mind. She'd been dying then, and her voice had been weak, but he'd heard her clearly. *You have to take care of each other. Stefan, will you promise? Promise to take care of each other?* And he had promised, and he would keep his word. No matter what.

"You know why I don't leave," he said again to Damon, who wouldn't look at him. "You can pretend you don't care. You can fool the whole world. But *I* know differently." It would have been kindest at this point to leave Damon alone, but Stefan wasn't in a kind mood. "You know that girl you picked up, Rachael?" he added. "The hair was all right, but her eyes were the wrong color. Elena's eyes were blue."

With that he turned, meaning to leave Damon here to think it over—if Damon would do anything so constructive, of course. But he never made it to the door.

"It's there!" said Meredith sharply, her eyes on the candle flame and the pin.

Bonnie sucked in her breath. Something was opening in front of her like a silver thread, a silver tunnel of communication. She was rushing along it, with no way to stop herself or check her speed. Oh, God, she thought, when I reach the end and hit—

The flash in Stefan's head was soundless, lightless, and powerful as a thunderclap. At the same time he felt a violent, wrenching tug. An urge to follow—something. This was not like Katherine's sly subliminal nudging to go somewhere; this was a psychic shout. A command that could not be disobeyed.

Inside the flash he sensed a presence, but he could scarcely believe who it was.

Bonnie?

Stefan! It's you! It worked!

Bonnie, what have you done?

Elena told me to. Honestly, Stefan, she did. We're in trouble and we need—

And that was it. The communication collapsed, caving in on itself, dwindling to a pinpoint. It was gone, and in its aftermath the room vibrated with Power.

Stefan and his brother were left staring at each other.

Bonnie let out a long breath she hadn't realized she'd been holding and opened her eyes, though she didn't remember closing them. She was lying on her back. Matt and Meredith were crouched over her, looking alarmed.

"What happened? Did it work?" Meredith demanded.

"It worked." She let them help her up. "I made contact with Stefan. I talked to him. Now all we can do is wait and see if he's coming or not."

"Did you mention Elena?" Matt asked.

"Yes."

"Then he's coming."

Five

Monday, June 8, 11:15 p.m.
Dear Diary,

I don't seem to be sleeping very well tonight, so I might as well write you. All day today I've been waiting for something to happen. You don't do a spell like that and have it work like that and then have nothing happen.

But nothing has. I stayed home from school because Mom thought I should. She was upset about Matt and Meredith staying so late Sunday night, and she said I needed to get some rest. But every time I lie down I see Sue's face.

Sue's dad did the eulogy at Elena's funeral. I wonder who's going to do it for Sue on Wednesday?

I've got to stop thinking about things like this.

Maybe I'll try to go to sleep again. Maybe if I lie down with my headphones on, I won't see Sue.

* * *

Bonnie put the diary back in her nightstand drawer and took out her Walkman. She flipped through the channels as she stared at the ceiling with heavy eyes. Through the crackle and sputter of static a D.J.'s voice sounded in her ear.

"And here's a golden oldie for all you fabulous fifties fans. 'Goodnight Sweetheart' on the Vee Jay label by The Spaniels . . ."

Bonnie drifted away on the music.

The ice cream soda was strawberry, Bonnie's favorite. The jukebox was playing 'Goodnight Sweetheart' and the counter was squeaky clean. But Elena, Bonnie decided, would never have really worn a poodle skirt.

"No poodles," she said, gesturing at it. Elena looked up from her hot fudge sundae. Her blond hair was pulled back in a ponytail. "Who thinks of these things anyway?" Bonnie asked.

"You do, silly. I'm only visiting."

"Oh." Bonnie took a pull at the soda. Dreams. There was a reason to be afraid of dreams, but she couldn't think of it just now.

"I can't stay long," Elena said. "I think he already knows I'm here. I just came to tell you . . ." She frowned.

Bonnie looked at her sympathetically. "Can't

you remember either?" She drank more soda. It tasted odd.

"I died too young, Bonnie. There was so much I was supposed to do, to accomplish. And now I have to help you."

"Thanks," Bonnie said.

"This isn't easy, you know. I don't have that much power. It's hard getting through, and it's hard keeping everything together."

"Gotta keep it together," Bonnie agreed, nodding. She was feeling strangely lightheaded. What was *in* this soda?

"I don't have much control, and things turn out strange somehow. He's doing it, I guess. He's always fighting me. He watches you. And every time we try to communicate, he comes."

"Okay." The room was floating.

"Bonnie, are you listening to me? He can use your fear against you. It's the way he gets in."

"Okay . . ."

"But *don't let him in*. Tell everyone that. And tell Stefan . . ." Elena stopped and put a hand to her mouth. Something fell onto the hot fudge sundae.

It was a tooth.

"He's here." Elena's voice was strange, indistinct. Bonnie stared at the tooth in mesmerized horror. It was lying in the middle of the whipped cream, among the slivered almonds. "Bonnie, tell Stefan . . ."

Another tooth plunked down, and another. Elena sobbed, both her hands at her mouth now. Her eyes were terrified, helpless. "Bonnie, don't go . . ."

But Bonnie was stumbling back. Everything was whirling around. The soda was bubbling out of the glass, but it wasn't soda; it was blood. Bright red and frothy, like something you coughed up when you died. Bonnie's stomach convulsed.

"Tell Stefan I love him!" It was the voice of a toothless old woman, and it ended in hysterical sobs. Bonnie was glad to fall into darkness and forget everything.

Bonnie nibbled at the end of her felt pen, her eyes on the clock, her mind on the calendar. Eight and a half more days of school to survive. And it looked as if every minute was going to be misery.

Some guy had said it outright, backing away from her on the stairs. "No offense, but your friends keep turning up dead." Bonnie had gone into the bathroom and cried.

But now all she wanted was to be out of school, away from the tragic faces and accusing eyes—or worse, the *pitying* eyes. The principal had given a speech over the P.A. about "this new misfortune" and "this terrible loss," and Bonnie had felt the eyes on her back as if they were boring holes there.

When the bell rang, she was the first person out the door. But instead of going to her next class she went to the bathroom again, where she waited for the next bell. Then, once the halls were empty, she hurried toward the foreign language wing. She passed bulletins and banners for end-of-the-year events without glancing at them. What did SATs matter, what did graduation matter, what did anything matter anymore? They might all be dead by the end of the month.

She nearly ran into the person standing in the hall. Her gaze jerked up, off her own feet, to take in fashionably ratty deck shoes, some foreign kind. Above that were jeans, body hugging, old enough to look soft over hard muscles. Narrow hips. Nice chest. Face to drive a sculptor crazy: sensuous mouth, high cheekbones. Dark sunglasses. Slightly tousled black hair. Bonnie stood gaping a moment.

Oh, my God, I forgot how gorgeous he is, she thought. Elena, forgive me; I'm going to grab him.

"Stefan!" she said.

Then her mind wrenched her back into reality again and she cast a hunted look around. No one was in eyeshot. She grabbed his arm.

"Are you crazy, showing up here? Are you *nuts?*"

"I had to find you. I thought it was urgent."

"It is, but—" He looked so incongruous, standing there in the high school hallway. So exotic. Like a zebra in a flock of sheep. She started pushing him toward a broom closet.

He wasn't going. And he was stronger than she was. "Bonnie, you said you'd talked to—"

"You have to hide! I'll go get Matt and Meredith and bring them back here and then we can talk. But if anybody sees you, you're probably going to get lynched. There's been another murder."

Stefan's face changed, and he let her push him toward the closet. He started to say something, then clearly decided not to.

"I'll wait," he said simply.

It took only a few minutes to find Matt in auto tech and Meredith in economics class. They hurried back to the broom closet and bustled Stefan out of school as inconspicuously as possible, which wasn't very.

Someone's bound to have seen us, Bonnie thought. It all depends on *who*, and how much of a blab they are.

"We have to get him someplace safe—not to

any of our houses," Meredith was saying. They were all walking as fast as they could through the high school parking lot.

"Fine, but *where*? Wait a minute, what about the boarding house . . . ?" Bonnie's voice trailed off. There was a little black car in the parking slot in front of her. An Italian car, sleek, svelte, and sexy looking. All the windows were tinted illegally dark; you couldn't even see inside. Then Bonnie made out the stallion emblem on the back.

"Oh, my *God*."

Stefan glanced at the Ferrari distractedly. "It's Damon's."

Three sets of eyes turned to him in shock. "*Damon's?*" Bonnie said, hearing the squeak in her own voice. She hoped Stefan meant Damon had just loaned it to him.

But the car window was rolling down to reveal black hair as sleek and liquidy as the car's paint job, mirrored glasses, and a very white smile. "*Buon giorno*," said Damon smoothly. "Anybody need a ride?"

"Oh, my God," Bonnie said again, faintly. But she didn't back away.

Stefan was visibly impatient. "We'll head for the boarding house. You follow. Park behind the barn so nobody sees your car."

Meredith had to lead Bonnie away from the

Ferrari. It wasn't that Bonnie liked Damon or that she was ever going to let him kiss her again as he had at Alaric's party. She knew he was dangerous; not as bad as Katherine had been, maybe, but bad. He'd killed wantonly, just for the fun of it. He'd killed Mr. Tanner, the history teacher, at the Haunted House fund-raiser last Halloween. He might kill again at any time. Maybe that was why Bonnie felt like a mouse staring at a shining black snake when she looked at him.

In the privacy of Meredith's car Bonnie and Meredith exchanged glances.

"Stefan shouldn't have brought him," said Meredith.

"Maybe he just came," Bonnie offered. She didn't think Damon was the sort of person who got *brought* anywhere.

"Why should he? Not to help us, that's for sure."

Matt said nothing. He didn't even seem to notice the tension in the car. He just stared through the windshield, lost in himself.

The sky was clouding up.

"Matt?"

"Just leave it alone; Bonnie," said Meredith.

Wonderful, thought Bonnie, depression settling like a dark blanket over her. Matt and Stefan and Damon, all together, all thinking about Elena.

They parked behind the old barn, next to the low black car. When they went inside, Stefan was standing alone. He turned and Bonnie saw that he'd taken off his sunglasses. The faintest chill went through her, just the lightest prickling of the hairs on her arms and neck. Stefan wasn't like any other guy she'd ever met. His eyes were so green; green as oak leaves in the spring. But just now they had shadows underneath.

There was a moment of awkwardness; the three of them standing on one side and looking at Stefan without a word. No one seemed to know what to say.

Then Meredith went over to him and took his hand. "You look tired," she said.

"I came as soon as I could." He put an arm around her in a brief, almost hesitant hug. He never would have done that in the old days, Bonnie thought. He used to be so reserved.

She came forward for her own hug. Stefan's skin was cool under the T-shirt, and she had to make herself not shiver. When she pulled back, her eyes were swimming. What did she feel now that Stefan Salvatore was back in Fell's Church? Relief? Sadness for the memories he brought with him? Fear? All she could tell was that she wanted to cry.

Stefan and Matt were looking at each other. Here we go, thought Bonnie. It was almost funny; the same expression was on both their faces. Hurt and tired, and trying not to show it. No matter what, Elena would always be between them.

At last, Matt stuck out his hand and Stefan shook it. They both stepped back, looking glad to have it over with.

"Where's Damon?" said Meredith.

"Poking around. I thought we might want a few minutes without him."

"We want a few *decades* without him," Bonnie said before she could stop herself, and Meredith said, "He can't be trusted, Stefan."

"I think you're wrong," Stefan said quietly. "He can be a big help if he puts his mind to it."

"In between killing a few of the locals every other night?" Meredith said, her eyebrows up. "You shouldn't have brought him, Stefan."

"But he didn't." The voice came from behind Bonnie, behind and frighteningly close. Bonnie jumped and made an instinctive lunge for Matt, who gripped her shoulder.

Damon smiled briefly, just one corner of his mouth up. He'd taken off his sunglasses, but his eyes weren't green. They were black as the spaces between the stars. He's almost better looking than Stefan, Bonnie thought wildly, finding Matt's fingers and hanging on to them.

"So she's yours now, is she?" Damon said to Matt casually.

"No," Matt said, but his grip on Bonnie didn't loosen.

"Stefan didn't bring you?" prompted Meredith from the other side. Of all of them, she seemed least affected by Damon, least afraid of him, least susceptible to him.

"No," Damon said, still looking at Bonnie. He doesn't *turn* like other people, she thought. He goes on looking at whatever he wants no matter who's talking. "You did," he said.

"Me?" Bonnie shrank a little, uncertain who he meant.

"You. You did the spell, didn't you?"

"The . . ." Oh, *hell*. A picture blossomed in Bonnie's mind, of black hair on a white napkin. Her eyes went to Damon's hair, finer and straighter than Stefan's but just as dark. Obviously Matt had made a mistake in the sorting.

Stefan's voice was impatient. "You sent for us, Bonnie. We came. What's going on?"

They took seats on the decaying bales of hay, all except Damon, who remained standing. Stefan was leaning forward, hands on knees, looking at Bonnie.

"You told me—you said that Elena spoke to

you." There was a perceptible pause before he got the name out. His face was tense with control.

"Yes." She managed a smile for him. "I had this dream, Stefan, this very strange dream . . ."

She told him about it, and about what had happened after. It took a long time. Stefan listened intently, his green eyes flaring every time she mentioned Elena. When she told about the end of Caroline's party and how they had found Sue's body in the backyard, the blood drained from his face, but he said nothing.

"The police came and said she was dead, but we knew that already," Bonnie finished. "And they took Vickie away—poor Vickie was just raving. They wouldn't let us talk to her, and her mother hangs up if we call. Some people are even saying Vickie *did* it, which is insane. But they won't believe that Elena talked to us, so they won't believe anything she said."

"And what she said was 'he,' " Meredith interrupted. "Several times. It's a man; someone with a lot of psychic power."

"And it was a man who grabbed my hand in the hallway," said Bonnie. She told Stefan about her suspicion of Tyler, but as Meredith pointed out, Tyler didn't fit the rest of the description.

He had neither the brains nor the psychic power to be the one Elena was warning them about.

"What about Caroline?" Stefan asked. "Could she have seen anything?"

"She was out front," Meredith said. "She found the door and got out while we were all running. She heard the screams, but she was too frightened to go back in the house. And to be honest, I don't blame her."

"So nobody actually saw what happened except Vickie."

"No. And Vickie's not telling." Bonnie picked up the story where she had left off. "Once we realized nobody would believe us, we remembered Elena's message about the summoning spell. We figured it must have been you she wanted to summon, because she thought you could do something to help. So . . . can you?"

"I can try," Stefan said. He got up and walked a little distance away, turning his back on them. He stood like that in silence a while, unmoving. At last he turned back and looked Bonnie in the eyes. "Bonnie," he said, quiet but intense, "in your dreams you actually spoke to Elena face to face. Do you think if you went into a trance you could do it again?"

Bonnie was a little frightened by what she saw in his eyes. They were blazing emerald green in his pale face. All at once it was as if she could see behind the mask of control he wore. Underneath was so much pain, so much longing—so much of that *intensity* that she could hardly bear to look at it.

"I *could*, maybe . . . but Stefan—"

"Then we'll do it. Right here, right now. And we'll see if you can take me with you." Those eyes were mesmerizing, not with any hidden Power, but with the sheer force of his will. Bonnie wanted to do it for him—he made her want to do anything for him. But the memory of that last dream was too much. She couldn't face that horror again; she *couldn't*.

"Stefan, it's too dangerous. I could be opening myself up to anything—and I'm *scared*. If that thing gets hold of my mind, I don't know what might happen. I *can't*, Stefan. Please. Even with a Ouija board, it's just inviting him to come."

For a moment she thought he was going to try to make her do it. His mouth tightened in an obstinate line, and his eyes blazed even brighter. But then, slowly, the fire died out of them.

Bonnie felt her heart tear. "Stefan, I'm sorry," she whispered.

"We'll just have to do it on our own," he said. The mask was back on, but his smile looked stiff, as if it hurt him. Then he spoke more briskly. "First we have to find out who this killer is, what he wants here. All we know now is that something evil has come to Fell's Church again."

"But *why*?" said Bonnie. "Why would anything evil just happen to pick here? Haven't we been through enough?"

"It does seem a bit of a strange coincidence," Meredith said drolly. "Why should we be so singularly blessed?"

"It's not coincidence," said Stefan. He got up and lifted his hands as if unsure how to start. "There are some places on this earth that are . . . different," he said. "That are full of psychic energy, either positive or negative, good or evil. Some of them have always been that way, like the Bermuda Triangle and Salisbury Plain, the place where they built Stonehenge. Others *become* that way, especially where a lot of blood has been shed." He looked at Bonnie.

"Unquiet spirits," she whispered.

"Yes. There was a battle here, wasn't there?"

"In the Civil War," Matt said. "That's how the church in the cemetery got ruined. It was a slaughter on both sides. Nobody won, but almost everyone who fought got killed. The woods are full of their graves."

"And the ground was soaked with blood. A place like that draws the supernatural to it. It draws evil to it. That's why Katherine was attracted to Fell's Church in the first place. I felt it too, when I first came here."

"And now something else has come," Meredith said, perfectly serious for once. "But how are we supposed to fight it?"

"We have to know what we're fighting first. I think . . ." But before he could finish, there was a creak and pale, dusty sunlight fell across the bales of hay. The barn door had opened.

Everyone tensed defensively, ready to jump up and run or fight. The figure nudging the huge door back with one elbow, however, was anything but menacing.

Mrs. Flowers, who owned the boarding house, smiled at them, her little black eyes crinkling into wrinkles. She was carrying a tray.

"I thought you children might like something to drink while you're talking," she said comfortably.

Everyone exchanged disconcerted glances. How had she known they were out here? And how could she be so calm about it?

"Here you go," Mrs. Flowers continued. "This is grape juice, made from my own Concord grapes." She put a paper cup beside Meredith, then Matt, then Bonnie. "And here are some gingersnap cookies. Fresh." She held the plate around. Bonnie noticed she didn't offer any to Stefan or Damon.

"You two can come round to the cellar if you like and try some of my blackberry wine," she said to them, with what Bonnie would swear was a wink.

Stefan took a deep, wary breath. "Uh, look, Mrs. Flowers . . ."

"And your old room's just like you left it. Nobody's been up there since you went. You can use it when you want; it won't put me out a bit."

Stefan seemed at a loss for words. "Well—thank you. Thank you very much. But—"

"If you're worried I'll say something to somebody, you can set your mind at ease. I don't tend to run off at the mouth. Never have, never will. How's that grape juice?"—turning suddenly on Bonnie.

Bonnie hastily took a gulp. "Good," she said truthfully.

"When you finish, throw the cups in the trash. I like things kept tidy." Mrs. Flowers cast a look about the barn, shaking her head and sighing. "Such a shame. Such a pretty girl." She looked at Stefan piercingly with eyes like onyx beads. "You've got your work cut out for you this time, boy," she said, and left, still shaking her head.

"Well!" said Bonnie, staring after her, amazed. Everyone else just looked at each other blankly.

" 'Such a pretty girl'—but which?" said Meredith at last. "Sue or Elena?" Elena had actually spent a week or so in this very barn last winter—but Mrs. Flowers wasn't supposed to know that. "Did *you* say something to her about us?" Meredith asked Damon.

"Not a word." Damon seemed amused. "She's an old lady. She's batty."

"She's sharper than any of us gave her credit for," Matt said. "When I think of the days we spent watching her potter around that basement—do you think she *knew* we were watching?"

"I don't know what to think," Stefan said slowly. "I'm just glad she seems to be on our side. And she's given us a safe place to stay."

"And grape juice, don't forget that." Matt grinned at Stefan. "Want some?" He proffered the leaky cup.

"Yeah, you can take your grape juice and . . ." But Stefan was almost smiling himself. For an instant Bonnie saw the two of them the way they used to be, before Elena had died. Friendly, warm, as comfortable together as she and Meredith were. A pang went through her.

But Elena isn't dead, she thought. She's more here than ever. She's directing everything we say and do.

Stefan had sobered again. "When Mrs. Flowers came in, I was about to say that we'd better get started. And I think we should start with Vickie."

"She won't see us," Meredith replied instantly. "Her parents are keeping everyone away."

"Then we'll just have to bypass her parents," Stefan said. "Are you coming with us, Damon?"

"A visit to yet another pretty girl? I wouldn't miss it."

Bonnie turned to Stefan in alarm, but he spoke reassuringly as he guided her out of the barn. "It'll be all right. I'll keep an eye on him."

Bonnie hoped so.

Six

Vickie's house was on a corner, and they approached it from the side street. By now the sky was filled with heavy purple clouds. The light had an almost underwater quality.

"Looks like it's going to storm," Matt said.

Bonnie glanced at Damon. Neither he nor Stefan liked bright light. And she could feel the Power emanating from him, like a low thrum just under the surface of his skin. He smiled without looking at her and said, "How about snow in June?"

Bonnie clamped down on a shiver.

She had looked Damon's way once or twice in the barn and found him listening to the story with an air of detached indifference. Unlike Stefan, his expression hadn't changed in the slightest when she mentioned Elena—or when she told about Sue's death. What did he really feel for Elena? He'd called up a snowstorm once and left her to freeze in it. What was he feeling now? Did he even care about catching the murderer?

"That's Vickie's bedroom," said Meredith. "The bay window in the back."

Stefan looked at Damon. "How many people in the house?"

"Two. Man and woman. The woman's drunk."

Poor Mrs. Bennett, thought Bonnie.

"I need them both asleep," Stefan said.

In spite of herself, Bonnie was fascinated by the surge of Power she felt from Damon. Her psychic abilities had never been strong enough to sense its raw essence before, but now they were. Now she could feel it as clearly as she could see the fading violet light or smell the honeysuckle outside Vickie's window.

Damon shrugged. "They're asleep."

Stefan tapped lightly on the glass.

There was no response, or at least none Bonnie could see. But Stefan and Damon looked at each other.

"She's half tranced already," Damon said.

"She's scared. I'll do it; she knows me," said Stefan. He put his fingertips on the window. "Vickie, it's Stefan Salvatore," he said. "I'm here to help you. Come let me in."

His voice was quiet, nothing that should have

been heard on the other side of the glass. But after a moment the curtains stirred and a face appeared.

Bonnie gasped aloud.

Vickie's long, light brown hair was disheveled, and her skin was chalky. There were huge black rings under her eyes. The eyes themselves were fixed and glassy. Her lips were rough and chapped.

"She looks like she's dressed up to do Ophelia's mad scene," Meredith said under her breath. "Nightgown and all."

"She looks *possessed*," Bonnie whispered back, unnerved.

Stefan just said, "Vickie, open the window."

Mechanically, like a windup doll, Vickie cranked one of the side panels of the bay window open, and Stefan said, "Can I come in?"

Vickie's glazed eyes swept over the group outside. For a moment Bonnie thought she didn't recognize any of them. But then she blinked and said slowly, "Meredith . . . Bonnie . . . Stefan? You're back. What are you doing here?"

"Ask me in, Vickie." Stefan's voice was hypnotic.

"Stefan . . ." There was a long pause and then: "Come in."

She stepped back as he put a hand on the sill and vaulted through. Matt followed him, then

Meredith. Bonnie, who was wearing a mini, remained outside with Damon. She wished she'd worn jeans to school today, but then she hadn't known she'd be going on an expedition.

"You shouldn't be here," Vickie said to Stefan, almost calmly. "He's coming to get me. He'll get you too."

Meredith put an arm around her. Stefan just said, "Who?"

"Him. He comes to me in my dreams. He killed Sue." Vickie's matter-of-fact tone was more frightening than any hysteria could have been.

"Vickie, we've come to help you," Meredith said gently. "Everything's going to be all right now. We won't let him hurt you, I promise."

Vickie swung around to stare at her. She looked Meredith up and down as if Meredith had suddenly changed into something unbelievable. Then she began to laugh.

It was awful, a hoarse burst of mirth like a hacking cough. It went on and on until Bonnie wanted to cover her ears. Finally Stefan said, "Vickie, stop it."

The laughter died into something like sobs, and when Vickie lifted her head again, she looked less glassy eyed but more genuinely upset. "You're all going to die, Stefan," she said, shaking her head. "No one can fight him and live."

"We need to know about him so we *can* fight him. We need your help," Stefan said. "Tell me what he looks like."

"I can't see him in my dreams. He's just a shadow without a face." Vickie whispered it, her shoulders hunching.

"But you saw him at Caroline's house," Stefan said insistently. "Vickie, listen to me," he added as the girl turned away sharply. "I know you're frightened, but this is important, more important than you can understand. We can't fight him unless we know what we're up against, and you are the only one, the *only* one right now who has the information we need. You have to help us."

"I can't *remember*—"

Stefan's voice was unyielding. "I have a way to help you remember," he said. "Will you let me try?"

Seconds crawled by, then Vickie gave a long, bubbling sigh, her body sagging. "Do whatever you want," she said indifferently. "I don't care. It won't make any difference."

"You're a brave girl. Now look at me, Vickie. I want you to relax. Just look at me and relax." Stefan's voice dropped to a lulling murmur. It went on for a few minutes, and then Vickie's eyes drooped shut.

"Sit down." Stefan guided her to sit on the bed. He sat beside her, looking into her face.

"Vickie, you feel calm and relaxed now. Nothing you remember will hurt you," he said, his voice soothing. "Now, I need you to go back to Saturday night. You're upstairs, in the master bedroom of Caroline's house. Sue Carson is with you, and someone else. I need you to see—"

"No!" Vickie twisted back and forth as if trying to escape something. "No! I can't—"

"Vickie, calm down. He won't hurt you. He can't see you, but you can see him. Listen to me."

As Stefan spoke, Vickie's whimpers quieted. But she still thrashed and writhed.

"You *need* to see him, Vickie. Help us fight him. What does he look like?"

"He looks like the devil!"

It was almost a scream. Meredith sat on Vickie's other side and took her hand. She looked out through the window at Bonnie, who looked back wide eyed and shrugged slightly. Bonnie had no idea what Vickie was talking about.

"Tell me more," Stefan said evenly.

Vickie's mouth twisted. Her nostrils were flared as if she were smelling something awful. When she spoke, she got out each word separately, as if they were making her sick.

"He wears . . . an old raincoat. It flaps around his legs in the wind. He makes the wind blow. His hair is blond. Almost white. It stands up all over his head. His eyes are so blue—electric blue." Vickie licked her lips and swallowed, looking nauseated. "Blue is the color of death."

Thunder rumbled and cracked in the sky. Damon glanced up quickly, then frowned, eyes narrowed.

"He's tall. And he's laughing. He's reaching for me, laughing. But Sue screams 'No, no' and tries to pull me away. So he takes her instead. The window's broken, and the balcony is right there. Sue's crying 'No, please.' And then I watch him—I watch him throw her . . ." Vickie's breath was hitching, her voice rising hysterically.

"Vickie, it's all right. You're not really there. You're safe."

"Oh, please, no—Sue! *Sue! Sue!*"

"Vickie, stay with me. Listen. I need just one more thing. Look at him. Tell me if he's wearing a blue jewel—"

But Vickie was whipping her head back and forth, sobbing, more hysterical each second. "No! No! I'm next! I'm next!" Suddenly, her eyes sprang open as she came out of the trance by herself, choking and gasping. Then her head jerked around.

On the wall, a picture was rattling.

It was picked up by the bamboo-framed mirror, then by perfume bottles and lipsticks on the dresser below. With a sound like popcorn, earrings began bursting from an earring tree. The rattling got louder and louder. A straw hat fell off a hook. Photos were showering down from the mirror. Tapes and CDs sprayed out of a rack and onto the floor like playing cards being dealt.

Meredith was on her feet and so was Matt, fists clenched.

"Make it stop! Make it stop!" Vickie cried wildly.

But it didn't stop. Matt and Meredith looked around as new objects joined the dance. Everything movable was shaking, jittering, swaying. It was as if the room were caught in an earthquake.

"Stop! Stop!" shrieked Vickie, her hands over her ears.

Directly above the house thunder exploded.

Bonnie jumped violently as she saw the zigzag of lightning shoot across the sky. Instinctively she grabbed for something to hang on to. As the lightning bolt flared a poster on Vickie's wall tore diagonally as if slashed by a phantom knife. Bonnie choked back a scream and clutched tighter.

Then, as quickly as if someone had flicked a power switch off, all the noise stopped.

Vickie's room was still. The fringe on the bedside lamp swayed slightly. The poster had curled up in two irregular pieces, top and bottom. Slowly, Vickie lowered her hands from her ears.

Matt and Meredith looked around rather shakily.

Bonnie shut her eyes and murmured something like a prayer. It wasn't until she opened them again that she realized what she had been hanging on to. It was the supple coolness of a leather jacket. It was Damon's arm.

He hadn't moved away from her, though. He didn't move now. He was leaning forward slightly, eyes narrowed, watching the room intently.

"Look at the mirror," he said.

Everyone did, and Bonnie drew in her breath, fingers clenching again. She hadn't seen it, but it must have happened while everything in the room was going berserk.

On the glass surface of the bamboo mirror two words were scrawled in Vickie's hot coral lipstick.

Goodnight, Sweetheart.

"Oh, God," Bonnie whispered.

Stefan turned from the mirror to Vickie. There was something different about him, Bonnie thought—he was holding himself relaxed but poised, like a soldier who's just gotten confirmation of a battle. It was as if he'd accepted a personal challenge of some kind.

He took something out of his back pocket and unfolded it, revealing sprigs of a plant with long green leaves and tiny lilac flowers.

"This is vervain, fresh vervain," he said quietly, his voice even and intense. "I picked it outside Florence; it's blooming there now." He took Vickie's hand and pressed the packet into it. "I want you to hold on to this and keep it. Put some in every room of the house, and hide pieces somewhere in your parents' clothes if you can, so they'll have it near them. As long as you have this with you, he can't take over your mind. He can scare you, Vickie, but he can't make you do anything, like open a window or door for him. And listen, Vickie, because this is important."

Vickie was shivering, her face crumpled. Stefan took both her hands and made her look at him, speaking slowly and distinctly.

"If I'm right, Vickie, *he can't get in unless you let him*. So talk to your parents. Tell them it's important that they don't ask any stranger inside the house. In fact, I can have Damon put that suggestion in their mind right now." He glanced at Damon, who shrugged slightly and nodded, looking as if his attention was somewhere else. Self-consciously, Bonnie removed her hand from his jacket.

Vickie's head was bent over the vervain.

"He'll get in somehow," she said softly, with terrible certainty.

"No. Vickie, listen to me. From now on, we're going to watch your house; we're going to be waiting for him."

"It doesn't *matter*," Vickie said. "You can't stop him." She began to laugh and cry at the same time.

"We're going to try," Stefan said. He looked at Meredith and Matt, who nodded. "Right. From this moment on, you will never be alone. There will always be one or more of us outside watching you."

Vickie just shook her bent head. Meredith gave her arm a squeeze and stood as Stefan tilted his head toward the window.

When she and Matt joined him there, Stefan spoke to all of them in a low voice. "I don't want to leave her unguarded, but I can't stay myself right now. There's something I have to do, and I need one of the girls with me. On the other hand, I don't want to leave either Bonnie or Meredith alone here." He turned to Matt. "Matt, will you . . ."

"I'll stay," said Damon.

Everyone looked at him, startled.

"Well, it's the logical solution, isn't it?" Damon seemed amused. "After all, what do you expect one of *them* to do against him anyway?"

"They can call for *me*. I can monitor their thoughts that far," Stefan said, not giving one inch.

"Well," Damon said whimsically, "I can call for you too, little brother, if I get into trouble. I'm getting bored with this investigation of yours anyway. I might as well stay here as anywhere."

"Vickie needs to be protected, not abused," Stefan said.

Damon's smile was charming. "*Her?*" He nodded toward the girl who sat on the bed, rocking over the vervain. From disheveled hair to bare feet, Vickie was not a pretty picture. "Take my word for it, brother, I can do better than that." For just an instant Bonnie thought those dark eyes flicked sideways toward her. "You're always saying how you'd like to trust me, anyway," Damon added. "Here's your chance to prove it."

Stefan looked as if he wanted to trust, as if he were tempted. He also looked suspicious. Damon said nothing, merely smiled in that taunting, enigmatic way. Practically asking to be *mistrusted*, Bonnie thought.

The two brothers stood looking at each other while the silence and the tension stretched out between them. Just then Bonnie could see the family resemblance in their faces, one serious and intense, the other bland and faintly mocking, but both inhumanly beautiful.

Stefan let his breath out slowly. "All right," he said quietly at last. Bonnie and Matt and Meredith were all staring at him, but he didn't seem to notice. He spoke to Damon as if they were the only two people there. "You stay here, outside the house where you won't be seen. I'll come back and take over when I'm finished with what I'm doing."

Meredith's eyebrows were in her hair, but she made no comment. Neither did Matt. Bonnie tried to quell her own feelings of unease. Stefan must know what he's doing, she told herself. Anyway, he'd *better*.

"Don't take too long," Damon said dismissively.

And that was how they left it, with Damon blending in with the darkness in the shadow of the black walnut trees in Vickie's backyard and Vickie herself in her room, rocking endlessly.

In the car, Meredith said, "Where next?"

"I need to test a theory," said Stefan briefly.

"That the killer is a vampire?" Matt said from the back, where he sat with Bonnie.

Stefan glanced at him sharply. "Yes."

"That's why you told Vickie not to invite anyone in," Meredith added, not to be outdone in the reasoning department. Vampires, Bonnie remembered, couldn't enter a place where humans lived and slept unless they were invited. "And that's why you asked if the man was wearing a blue stone."

"An amulet against daylight," Stefan said, spreading his right hand. On the third finger there was a silver ring set with lapis lazuli. "Without one of these, direct exposure to the sun kills us. If the murderer *is* a vampire, he keeps a stone like this somewhere on him." As if by instinct, Stefan reached up to briefly touch something under his T-shirt. After a moment Bonnie realized what it must be.

Elena's ring. Stefan had given it to her in the first place, and after she died he'd taken it to wear on a chain around his neck. So that part of her would be with him always, he'd said.

When Bonnie looked at Matt beside her, she saw his eyes were closed.

"So how can we tell if he's a vampire?" Meredith asked.

"There's only one way I can think of, and it isn't very pleasant. But it's got to be done."

Bonnie's heart sank. If Stefan thought it wasn't very pleasant, she was sure she was going to find it even less so. "What is it?" she said unenthusiastically.

"I need to get a look at Sue's body."

There was dead silence. Even Meredith, normally so unflappable, looked appalled. Matt turned away, leaning his forehead against the window glass.

"You've got to be kidding," Bonnie said.

"I wish I were."

"But—for God's sake, Stefan. We *can't*. They won't let us. I mean, what are we going to say? 'Excuse me while I examine this corpse for holes'?"

"Bonnie, stop it," Meredith said.

"I can't help it," Bonnie snapped back shakily. "It's an *awful* idea. And besides, the police already checked her body. There wasn't a mark on it except the cuts she got in the fall."

"The police don't know what to look for," Stefan said. His voice was steely. Hearing it brought something home to Bonnie, something she tended to forget. Stefan was one of *them*. One of the hunters. He'd seen dead people before. He might even have killed some.

He drinks *blood*, she thought, and shuddered.

"Well?" said Stefan. "Are you still with me?"

Bonnie tried to make herself small in the backseat. Meredith's hands were tight on the steering wheel. It was Matt who spoke, turning back from the window.

"We don't have a choice, do we?" he said tiredly.

"There's a viewing of the body from seven to

ten at the funeral home," Meredith added, her voice low.

"We'll have to wait until after the viewing, then. After they close the funeral home, when we can be alone with her," said Stefan.

"This is the most gruesome thing I've ever had to do," Bonnie whispered wretchedly. The funeral chapel was dark and cold. Stefan had sprung the locks on the outside door with a thin piece of flexible metal.

The viewing room was thickly carpeted, its walls covered with somber oak panels. It would have been a depressing place even with the lights on. In the dark it seemed close and suffocating and crowded with grotesque shapes. It looked as if someone might be crouching behind each of the many standing flower arrangements.

"I don't want to *be* here," Bonnie moaned.

"Let's just get it over with, okay?" Matt said through his teeth.

When he snapped the flashlight on, Bonnie looked anywhere but where it was pointing. She didn't want to see the coffin, she *didn't*. She stared at the flowers, at a heart made of pink roses. Outside, thunder grumbled like a sleeping animal.

"Let me get this open—here," Stefan was saying. In spite of her resolve not to, Bonnie looked.

The casket was white, lined with pale pink satin. Sue's blond hair shone against it like the hair of a sleeping princess in a fairy tale. But Sue didn't look as if she were sleeping. She was too pale, too still. Like a waxwork.

Bonnie crept closer, her eyes fixed on Sue's face.

That's why it's so cold in here, she told herself staunchly. To keep the wax from melting. It helped a little.

Stefan reached down to touch Sue's high-necked pink blouse. He undid the top button.

"For God's *sake*," Bonnie whispered, outraged.

"What do you think we're here for?" Stefan hissed back. But his fingers paused on the second button.

Bonnie watched a minute and then made her decision. "Get out of the way," she said, and when Stefan didn't move immediately, she gave him a shove. Meredith drew up close to her and they formed a phalanx between Sue and the boys. Their eyes met with understanding. If they had to actually remove the blouse, the guys were going out.

Bonnie undid the small buttons while Meredith held the light. Sue's skin felt as waxy as it looked, cool against her fingertips. Awkwardly, she folded the blouse back to reveal a lacy white slip. Then she made herself push Sue's shining gold hair off the pale neck. The hair was stiff with spray.

"No holes," she said, looking at Sue's throat. She was proud that her voice was almost steady.

"No," said Stefan oddly. "But there's something else. Look at this." Gently, he reached around Bonnie to point out a cut, pale and bloodless as the skin around it, but visible as a faint line running from collarbone to breast. Over the heart. Stefan's long finger traced the air above it and Bonnie stiffened, ready to smack the hand away if he touched.

"What is it?" asked Meredith, puzzled.

"A mystery," Stefan said. His voice was still odd. "If I saw a mark like that on a vampire, it would mean the vampire was giving blood to a human. That's how it's done. Human teeth can't pierce our skin, so we cut ourselves if we want to share blood. But Sue wasn't a vampire."

"She certainly wasn't!" said Bonnie. She tried to fight off the image her mind wanted to show her, of Elena bending to a cut like that on Stefan's chest and sucking, drinking . . .

She shuddered and realized her eyes were shut. "Is there anything else you need to see?" she said, opening them.

"No. That's all."

Bonnie did up the buttons. She rearranged Sue's hair. Then, while Meredith and Stefan eased the lid of the casket back down, she walked quickly out of the viewing room and to the outside door. She stood there, arms wrapped around herself.

A hand touched her elbow lightly. It was Matt.

"You're tougher than you look," he said.

"Yes, well . . ." She tried to shrug. And then suddenly she was crying, crying hard. Matt put his arms around her.

"I know," he said. Just that. Not "Don't cry" or "Take it easy" or "Everything's going to be all right." Just "I know." His voice was as desolate as she felt.

"They've got hair spray in her hair," she sobbed. "Sue *never* used hair spray. It's awful." Somehow, just then, this seemed the worst thing of all.

He simply held her.

After a while Bonnie got her breath. She found she was holding on to Matt almost painfully tightly and loosened her arms. "I got your shirt all wet," she said apologetically, sniffling.

"It doesn't matter."

Something in his voice made her step back and look at him. He looked the way he had in the high school parking lot. So lost, so . . . hopeless.

"Matt, what is it?" she whispered. "Please."

"I told you already," he said. He was looking away into some immeasurable distance. "Sue's lying in there dead, and she shouldn't be. You said it yourself, Bonnie. What kind of world is it that lets a thing like that happen? That lets a girl like Sue get murdered for kicks, or kids in Afghanistan starve, or baby seals get skinned alive? If that's what the world is like, what does anything matter? It's all over anyway." He paused and seemed to come back to himself. "Do you understand what I'm talking about?"

"I'm not so sure." Bonnie didn't even think she wanted to. It was too scary. But she was overwhelmed by an urge to comfort him, to wipe that lost look from his eyes. "Matt, I—"

"We're finished," Stefan said from behind them.

As Matt looked toward the voice the lost look seemed to intensify. "Sometimes I think we're *all* finished," Matt said, moving away from Bonnie, but he didn't explain what he meant by that. "Let's go."

Seven

Stefan approached the corner house reluctantly, almost afraid of what he might find. He half expected that Damon would have abandoned his post by now. He'd probably been an idiot to rely on Damon in the first place.

But when he reached the backyard, there was a shimmer of motion among the black walnut trees. His eyes, sharper than a human's because they were adapted for hunting, made out the darker shadow leaning against a trunk.

"You took your time getting back."

"I had to see the others home safe. And I had to eat."

"Animal blood," Damon said contemptuously, eyes fixed on a tiny round stain on Stefan's T-shirt. "Rabbit, from the smell of it. That seems appropriate somehow, doesn't it?"

"Damon—I've given Bonnie and Meredith vervain too."

"A wise precaution," Damon said distinctly, and showed his teeth.

A familiar surge of irritation welled up in Stefan. Why did Damon always have to be so difficult? Talking with him was like walking between land mines.

"I'll be going now," Damon continued, swinging his jacket over one shoulder. "I've got business of my own to take care of." He tossed a devastating grin over his shoulder. "Don't wait up."

"Damon." Damon half turned, not looking but listening. "The last thing we need is some girl in this town screaming 'Vampire!' " Stefan said. "Or showing the signs, either. These people have been through it before; they're not ignorant."

"I'll bear that in mind." It was said ironically, but it was the closest thing to a promise Stefan had ever gotten from his brother in his life.

"And, Damon?"

"Now what?"

"Thank you."

It was too much. Damon whipped around, his eyes cold and uninviting, a stranger's eyes.

"Don't expect anything of me, little brother," he said dangerously. "Because you'll be wrong every time. And don't think you can manipulate me, either. Those three humans may follow you, but I won't. I'm here for reasons of my own."

He was gone before Stefan could gather words for a reply. It wouldn't have mattered anyway. Damon never listened to anything he said. Damon never even called him by name. It was always the scornful "little brother."

And now Damon was off to prove how unreliable he was, Stefan thought. Wonderful. He'd do something particularly vicious just to show Stefan he was capable of it.

Wearily, Stefan found a tree to lean against and slid down it to look at the night sky. He tried to think about the problem at hand, about what he'd learned tonight. The description Vickie had given of the killer. Tall, blond hair and blue eyes, he thought—that seemed to remind him of someone. Not someone he'd met, but someone he'd heard about . . .

It was no use. He couldn't keep his mind on the puzzle. He was tired and lonely and in desperate need of comfort. And the stark truth was that there was no comfort to be had.

Elena, he thought, you lied to me.

It was the one thing she'd insisted on, the one thing she'd always promised. "Whatever happens, Stefan, I'll be with you. Tell me you believe that." And he had answered, helpless in her spell, "Oh, Elena, I believe it. Whatever happens, we'll be together."

But she had left him. Not by choice maybe, but what did that matter in the end? She had left him and gone away.

There were times when all he wanted was to follow her.

Think about something else, anything else, he told himself, but it was too late. Once unleashed, the images of Elena swirled around him, too painful to bear, too beautiful to push away.

The first time he'd kissed her. The shock of dizzy sweetness when his mouth met hers. And after that, shock after shock, but at some deeper level. As if she were reaching down to the core of himself, a core he'd almost forgotten.

Frightened, he'd felt his defenses tear away. All his secrets, all his resistance, all the tricks he used to keep other people at arm's length. Elena had ripped through them all, exposing his vulnerability.

Exposing his soul.

And in the end, he found that it was what he wanted. He wanted Elena to see him without defenses, without walls. He wanted her to know him for what he was.

Terrifying? Yes. When she'd discovered his secret at last, when she'd found him feeding on that bird, he had cringed in shame. He was sure that she'd turn away from the blood on his mouth in horror. In disgust.

But when he looked into her eyes that night, he saw understanding. Forgiveness. Love.

Her love had healed him.

And that was when he knew they could never be apart.

Other memories surged up and Stefan held on to them, even though the pain tore into him like claws. Sensations. The feel of Elena against him, supple in his arms. The brush of her hair on his cheek, light as a moth's wing. The curve of her lips, the taste of them. The impossible midnight blue of her eyes.

All lost. All beyond his reach forever.

But Bonnie had reached Elena. Elena's spirit, her soul, was still somewhere near.

Of anyone, he should be able to summon it. He had Power at his command. And he had more right than anyone to seek her.

He knew how it was done. Shut your eyes. Picture the person you want to draw near. That was easy. He could see Elena, feel her, smell her. Then call them, let your longing reach out into the emptiness. Open yourself and let your need be felt.

Easier still. He didn't give a damn about the danger. He gathered all his yearning, all his pain, and sent it out searching like a prayer.

And felt . . . nothing.

Only void and his own loneliness. Only silence.

His Power wasn't the same as Bonnie's. He couldn't reach the one thing he loved most, the one thing that mattered to him.

He had never felt so alone in his life.

"You want *what*?" Bonnie said.

"Some sort of records about the history of Fell's Church. Particularly about the founders," Stefan said. They were all sitting in Meredith's car, which was parked a discreet distance behind Vickie's house. It was dusk of the next day and they had just returned from Sue's funeral—all but Stefan.

"This has something to do with Sue, doesn't it?" Meredith's dark eyes, always so level and intelligent, probed Stefan's. "You think you've solved the mystery."

"Possibly," he admitted. He had spent the day thinking. He'd put the pain of last night behind him, and once again he was in control. Although he could not reach Elena, he could justify her faith in him—he could do what she wanted done. And there was a comfort in work, in concentration. In keeping all emotion away. He added, "I have an idea about what might have happened, but it's a long shot and I don't want to talk about it until I'm sure."

"Why?" demanded Bonnie. Such a contrast to Meredith, Stefan thought. Hair as red as fire and a spirit to go with it. That delicate heart-shaped face and fair, translucent skin were deceptive, though. Bonnie was smart and resourceful—even if she was only beginning to find that out herself.

"Because if I'm wrong, an innocent person might get hurt. Look, at this point it's just an idea. But I promise if I find any evidence tonight to back it up, I'll tell you all about it."

"You could talk with Mrs. Grimesby," Meredith suggested. "She's the town librarian, and she knows a lot about the founding of Fell's Church."

"Or there's always Honoria," Bonnie said. "I mean, she *was* one of the founders."

Stefan looked at her quickly. "I thought Honoria Fell had stopped communicating with you," he said carefully.

"I don't mean talk to *her*. She's gone, *pfft*, kaput," Bonnie said disgustedly. "I mean her journal. It's right there in the library with Elena's; Mrs. Grimesby has them on display near the circulation desk."

Stefan was surprised. He didn't entirely like the idea of Elena's journal on display. But Honoria's records might be exactly what he was looking for. Honoria had not just been a wise woman; she had been well versed in the supernatural. A witch.

"The library's closed by now, though," Meredith said.

"That's even better," said Stefan. "No one will know what information we're interested in. Two of us can go down there and break in, and the other two can stay here. Meredith, if you'll come with me—"

"I'd like to stay here, if you don't mind," she said. "I'm tired," she added in explanation, seeing his expression. "And this way I can get my watch over with and get home earlier. Why don't you and Matt go and Bonnie and I stay here?"

Stefan was still looking at her. "Okay," he said slowly. "Fine. If it's all right with Matt." Matt shrugged. "That's it, then. It might take us a couple of hours or more. You two stay in the car with the doors locked. You should be safe enough that way." If he was right in his suspicions, there wouldn't be any more attacks for a while—a few days at least. Bonnie and Meredith *should* be safe. But he couldn't help wonder what was behind Meredith's suggestion. Not simple tiredness, he was sure.

"By the way, where's Damon?" Bonnie asked as he and Matt started to leave.

Stefan felt his stomach muscles tighten. "I don't know." He had been waiting for someone to ask that. He hadn't seen his brother since last night, and he had no idea what Damon might be doing.

"He'll show up eventually," he said, and closed the door on Meredith's, "That's what I'm afraid of."

He and Matt walked to the library in silence, keeping to the shadows, skirting areas of light. He couldn't afford to be seen. Stefan had come back to help Fell's Church, but he felt sure Fell's Church didn't want his help. He was a stranger again, an intruder here. They would hurt him if they caught him.

The library lock was easy to pick, just a simple spring mechanism. And the journals were right where Bonnie had said they would be.

Stefan forced his hand away from Elena's journal. Inside was the record of Elena's last days, in her own handwriting. If he started thinking about that now . . .

He concentrated on the leather-bound book beside it. The faded ink on the yellowing pages was hard to read, but after a few minutes his eyes got accustomed to the dense, intricate writing with its elaborate curlicues.

It was the story of Honoria Fell and her husband, who with the Smallwoods and a few other families had come to this place when it was still virgin wilderness. They had faced not only the dangers of isolation and hunger but of native wildlife. Honoria told the story of their battle to survive simply and clearly, without sentimentality.

And in those pages Stefan found what he was looking for.

With a prickling at the back of his neck, he reread the entry carefully. At last he leaned back and shut his eyes.

He'd been right. There was no longer any doubt in his mind. And that meant he must also be right about what was going on in Fell's Church now. For an instant, bright sickness washed over him, and an anger that made him want to rip and tear and hurt something. Sue. Pretty Sue who had been Elena's friend had died for . . . that. A blood ritual, an obscene initiation. It made him want to *kill*.

But then the rage faded, replaced by a fierce determination to stop what was happening and set things right.

I promise you, he whispered to Elena in his own mind. I *will* stop it somehow. No matter what.

He looked up to find Matt looking at him.

Elena's journal was in Matt's hand, closing itself over his thumb. Just then Matt's eyes looked as dark a blue as Elena's. Too dark, full of turmoil and grief and something like bitterness.

"You found it," Matt said. "And it's bad."

"Yes."

"It would be." Matt pushed Elena's journal back into the case and stood. There was a ring almost of satisfaction in his voice. Like somebody who's just proved a point.

"I could have saved you the trouble of coming here." Matt surveyed the darkened library, jingling change in his pocket. A casual observer might have thought he was relaxed, but his voice betrayed him. It was raw with strain. "You just think of the worst thing you can imagine and that's always the truth," he said.

"Matt . . ." Sudden concern stabbed at Stefan. He'd been too preoccupied since coming back to Fell's Church to look at Matt properly. Now he realized that he'd been unforgivably stupid. Something was terribly wrong. Matt's whole body was rigid with tension lying just under the surface. And Stefan could sense the anguish, the desperation in his mind.

"Matt, what is it?" he said quietly. He got up and crossed to the other boy. "Is it something I did?"

"I'm fine."

"You're shaking." It was true. Fine tremors were running through the taut muscles.

"I said I'm fine!" Matt swung away from him, shoulders hunched defensively. "Anyway, what could *you* have done to upset me? Besides taking my girl and getting her killed, I mean?"

This stab was different, it was somewhere around Stefan's heart and it went straight through. Like the blade that had killed him once upon a time. He tried to breathe around it, not trusting himself to speak.

"I'm sorry." Matt's voice was leaden, and when Stefan looked, he saw that the tense shoulders had slumped. "That was a lousy thing to say."

"It was the truth." Stefan waited a moment and then added, levelly, "But it's not the whole problem, is it?"

Matt didn't answer. He stared at the floor, pushing something invisible with the side of one shoe. Just when Stefan was about to give up, he turned with a question of his own.

"What's the world really like?"

"What's . . . what?"

"The world. You've seen a lot of it, Stefan. You've got four or five centuries on the rest of us, right? So what's the deal? I mean, is it basically the kind of place worth saving or is it essentially a pile of crap?"

Stefan shut his eyes. "Oh."

"And what about people, huh, Stefan? The human race. Are we the disease or just a symptom? I mean, you take somebody like—like Elena." Matt's voice shook briefly, but he went on. "Elena died to keep the town safe for girls like Sue. And now Sue's dead. And it's all happening again. It's never over. We can't win. So what does that tell you?"

"Matt."

"What I'm really asking is, what's the point? Is there some cosmic joke I'm not getting? Or is the whole thing just one big freaking mistake? Do you understand what I'm trying to say here?"

"I understand, Matt." Stefan sat down and ran his hands through his hair. "If you'll shut up a minute, I'll try to answer you."

Matt drew up a chair and straddled it. "Great. Take your best shot." His eyes were hard and challenging, but underneath Stefan saw the bewildered hurt that had been festering there.

"I've seen a lot of evil, Matt, more than you can imagine," Stefan said. "I've even lived it. It's always going to be a part of me, no matter how I fight it. Sometimes I think the whole human race is evil, much less my kind. And sometimes I think that enough of both our races is evil that it doesn't matter what happens to the rest.

"When you get down to it, though, I don't

know any more than you do. I can't tell you if there's a point or if things are ever going to turn out all right." Stefan looked straight into Matt's eyes and spoke deliberately. "But I've got another question for you. So what?"

Matt stared. "So what?"

"Yeah. So what."

"So what if the universe is evil and if nothing we do to try and change it can really make any difference?" Matt's voice was gaining volume with his disbelief.

"Yeah, so what?" Stefan leaned forward. "So what are you going to do, Matt Honeycutt, if every bad thing you've said is true? What are you going to do personally? Are you going to stop fighting and swim with the sharks?"

Matt was grasping the back of his chair. "What are you talking about?"

"You can do that, you know. Damon says so all the time. You can join up with the evil side, the winning side. And nobody can really blame you, because if the universe is that way, why shouldn't you be that way too?"

"Like hell!" Matt exploded. His blue eyes were searing and he had half risen from his chair. "That's Damon's way, maybe! But just because it's hopeless doesn't mean it's all right to stop fighting. Even if I *knew* it was hopeless, I'd still have to try. I have to try, damn it!"

"I know." Stefan settled back and smiled faintly. It was a tired smile, but it showed the kinship he felt right then with Matt. And in a moment he saw by Matt's face that Matt understood.

"I know because I feel the same way," Stefan continued. "There's no excuse for giving up just because it looks like we're going to lose. We have to try—because the other choice is to surrender."

"I'm not ready to surrender *anything*," Matt said through his teeth. He looked as if he'd fought his way back to a fire inside him that had been burning all along. "Ever," he said.

"Yeah, well, 'ever' is a long time," Stefan said. "But for what it's worth, I'm going to try not to either. I don't know if it's possible, but I'm going to try."

"That's all anybody can do," Matt said. Slowly, he pushed himself off the chair and stood straight. The tension was gone from his muscles, and his eyes were the clear, almost piercing blue eyes Stefan remembered. "Okay," he said quietly. "If you found what you came for, we'd better get back to the girls."

Stefan thought, his mind switching gears. "Matt, if I'm right about what's going on, the girls should be okay for a while. But you go ahead and take over the watch from them. As long as I'm here there's something I'd like to read up on—by a guy named Gervase of Tilbury, who lived in the early 1200s."

"Even before your time, eh?" Matt said, and Stefan gave him the ghost of a smile. They stood for a moment, looking at each other.

"All right. I guess I'll see you at Vickie's." Matt turned to the door, then hesitated. Abruptly, he turned again and held out his hand. "Stefan—I'm glad you came back."

Stefan gripped it. "I'm glad to hear it" was all he said, but inside he felt a warmth that took away the stabbing pain.

And some of the loneliness, too.

Eight

From where Bonnie and Meredith sat in the car, they could just see Vickie's window. It would have been better to be closer, but then someone might have discovered them.

Meredith poured the last of the coffee out of the thermos and drank it. Then she yawned. She caught herself guiltily and looked at Bonnie.

"You having trouble sleeping at night too?"

"Yes. I can't imagine why," Meredith said.

"Do you think the guys are having a little talk?"

Meredith glanced at her quickly, obviously surprised, then smiled. Bonnie realized Meredith hadn't expected her to catch on. "I hope so," Meredith said. "It might do Matt some good."

Bonnie nodded and relaxed back into the

seat. Meredith's car had never seemed so comfortable before.

When she looked at Meredith again, the dark-haired girl was asleep.

Oh, great. Terrific. Bonnie stared into the dregs of her coffee mug, making a face. She didn't dare relax again; if they *both* fell asleep, it could be disastrous. She dug her nails into her palms and stared at Vickie's lighted window.

When she found the image blurring and doubling on her, she knew something had to be done.

Fresh air. That would help. Without bothering to be too quiet about it, she unlocked the door and pulled the handle up. The door clicked open, but Meredith went on breathing deeply.

She must really be tired, Bonnie thought, getting out. She shut the door more gently, locking Meredith inside. It was only then that she realized she herself didn't have a key.

Oh, well, she'd wake Meredith to let her back in. Meanwhile she'd go check on Vickie. Vickie was probably still awake.

The sky was brooding and overcast, but the night was warm. Behind Vickie's house the black walnut trees stirred very faintly. Crickets sang, but their monotonous chirping only seemed like part of a larger silence.

The scent of honeysuckle filled Bonnie's nostrils. She tapped on Vickie's window lightly with her fingernails, peering through the crack in the curtains.

No answer. On the bed she could make out a lump of blankets with unkempt brown hair sticking out the top. Vickie was asleep too.

As Bonnie stood there, the silence seemed to thicken around her. The crickets weren't singing anymore, and the trees were still. And yet it was as if she was straining to hear something she *knew* was there.

I'm not alone, she realized.

None of her ordinary senses told her this. But her sixth sense, the one that sent chills up her arms and ice down her spine, the one that was newly awakened to the presence of Power, was certain. There was . . . something . . . near. Something . . . watching her.

She turned slowly, afraid to make a sound. If she didn't make any noise, maybe whatever it was wouldn't get her. Maybe it wouldn't notice her.

The silence had become deadly, menacing. It hummed in her ears with the beat of her own blood. And she couldn't help imagining what might come screaming out of it at any minute.

Something with hot, moist hands, she thought, staring into the darkness of the backyard. Black on gray, black on black was all she could see. Every shape might be anything, and all the shadows seemed to be moving. Something with hot, sweaty hands and arms strong enough to crush her—

The snap of a twig exploded through her like gunfire.

She spun toward it, eyes and ears straining. But there was only darkness and silence.

Fingers touched the back of her neck.

Bonnie whirled again, almost falling, almost fainting. She was too frightened to scream. When she saw who it was, shock robbed all her senses and her muscles collapsed. She would have ended up in a heap on the ground if he hadn't caught her and held her straight.

"You look frightened," Damon said softly.

Bonnie shook her head. She didn't have any voice yet. She thought she still might faint. But she tried to pull away just the same.

He didn't tighten his grip, but he didn't let go. And struggling did about as much good as trying to break a brick wall with bare hands. She gave up and tried to calm her breathing.

"Are you frightened of *me?*" Damon said. He smiled reprovingly, as if they shared a secret. "You don't need to be."

How had Elena managed to deal with this? But Elena hadn't, of course, Bonnie realized.

Elena had succumbed to Damon in the end. Damon had won and had his way.

He released one of her arms to trace, very lightly, the curve of her upper lip. "I suppose I should go away," he said, "and not scare you anymore. Is that what you want?"

Like a rabbit with a snake, Bonnie thought. This is how the rabbit feels. Only I don't suppose he'll kill me. I might just die on my own, though. She felt as if her legs might melt away at any minute, as if she might collapse. There was a warmth and a trembling inside her.

Think of something . . . fast. Those unfathomable black eyes were filling the universe now. She thought she could see stars inside them. *Think*. Quickly.

Elena wouldn't like it, she thought, just as his lips touched hers. Yes, that was it. But the problem was, she didn't have the strength to say it. The warmth was growing, rushing out to all parts of her, from her fingertips to the soles of her feet. His lips were cool, like silk, but everything else was so warm. She didn't need to be afraid; she could just let go and float on this. Sweetness rushed through her . . .

"What the *hell* is going on?"

The voice broke the silence, broke the spell. Bonnie started and found herself able to turn her head. Matt was standing at the edge of the yard, his fists clenched, his eyes like chips of blue ice. Ice so cold it burned.

"Get away from her," Matt said.

To Bonnie's surprise, the grip on her arms eased. She stepped back, straightening her blouse, a little breathless. Her mind was working again.

"It's okay," she said to Matt, her voice almost normal. "I was just—"

"Go back to the car and stay there."

Now *wait* a minute, thought Bonnie. She was glad Matt had come; the interruption had been very conveniently timed. But he was coming on a little heavy with the protective older brother bit.

"Look, Matt—"

"Go on," he said, still staring at Damon.

Meredith wouldn't have let herself be ordered around this way. And Elena certainly wouldn't. Bonnie opened her mouth to tell Matt to go sit in the car himself when she suddenly realized something.

This was the first time in months she'd seen Matt really *care* about anything. The light was back in those blue eyes—that cold flash of righteous anger that used to make even Tyler Smallwood back down. Matt was alive right now, and full of energy. He was himself again.

Bonnie bit her lip. For a moment she struggled with her pride. Then she conquered it and lowered her eyes.

"Thanks for rescuing me," she murmured, and left the yard.

Matt was so angry he didn't dare move closer to Damon for fear he might take a swing at him. And the chilling darkness in Damon's eyes told him that wouldn't be a very good idea.

But Damon's voice was smooth, almost dispassionate. "My taste for blood isn't just a whim, you know. It's a necessity you're interfering with here. I'm only doing what I have to."

This callous indifference was too much for Matt. They think of us as food, he remembered. They're the hunters, we're the prey. And he had his claws in Bonnie, Bonnie who couldn't wrestle a kitten.

Contemptuously he said, "Why don't you pick on somebody your own size, then?"

Damon smiled and the air went colder. "Like you?"

Matt just stared at him. He could feel muscles clench in his jaw. After a moment he said tightly, "You can try."

"I can do more than try, Matt." Damon took a single step toward him like a stalking panther. Involuntarily, Matt thought of jungle cats, of their powerful spring and their sharp, tearing teeth. He thought of what Tyler had looked like in the Quonset hut last year when Stefan was through with him. Red meat. Just red meat and blood.

"What was that history teacher's name?" Damon was saying silkily. He seemed amused now, enjoying this. "Mr. Tanner, wasn't it? I did more than try with him."

"You're a murderer."

Damon nodded, unoffended, as if he'd just been introduced. "Of course, he stuck a knife in me. I wasn't planning to drain him quite dry, but he annoyed me and I changed my mind. You're annoying me now, Matt."

Matt had his knees locked to keep from running. It was more than the catlike stalking grace, it was more than those unearthly black eyes fastened on his. There was something *inside* Damon that whispered terror to the human brain. Some menace that spoke directly to Matt's blood, telling him to do anything to get away.

But he wouldn't run. His conversation with Stefan was blurred in his mind right now, but he knew one thing from it. Even if he died here, he wouldn't run.

"Don't be stupid," Damon said, as if he'd heard every word of Matt's thoughts. "You've never had blood taken from you by force, have you? It hurts, Matt. It hurts a lot."

Elena, Matt remembered. That first time when she'd taken his blood he'd been scared, and the fear had been bad enough. But he'd been doing it of his own volition then. What would it be like when he was unwilling?

I will not run. I will not look away.

Aloud he said, still looking straight at Damon, "If you're going to kill me, you'd better stop talking and do it. Because maybe you can make me die, but that's all you can make me do."

"You're even stupider than my brother," Damon said. With two steps he crossed the distance to Matt. He grabbed Matt by his T-shirt, one hand on either side of the throat. "I guess I'll have to teach you the same way."

Everything was frozen. Matt could smell his own fear, but he wouldn't move. He couldn't move now.

It didn't matter. He hadn't given in. If he died right now, he died knowing that.

Damon's teeth were a white glitter in the dark. Sharp as carving knives. Matt could almost feel the razor bite of them before they touched him.

I will not surrender anything, he thought, and closed his eyes.

The shove took him completely off balance. He stumbled and fell backward, his eyes flying open. Damon had let go and pushed him away.

Expressionless, those black eyes looked down at him where he sat in the dirt.

"I'll try to put this in a way you can understand," Damon said. "You don't want to mess with me, Matt. I am more dangerous than you can possibly imagine. Now get out of here. It's my watch."

Silently, Matt got up. He rubbed at his shirt where Damon's hands had crumpled it. And then he left, but he didn't run and he didn't flinch from Damon's eyes.

I won, he thought. I'm still alive, so I won.

And there had been a kind of grim respect in those black eyes in the end. It made Matt wonder about some things. It really did.

Bonnie and Meredith were sitting in the car when he got back. They both looked concerned.

"You were gone a long time," Bonnie said. "Are you okay?"

Matt wished people would stop asking him that. "I'm fine," he said, and then added, "Really." After a moment's thought he decided there was something else he should say. "Sorry if I yelled at you back there, Bonnie."

"That's all right," Bonnie said coolly. Then, thawing, she said, "You really do look better, you know. More like your old self."

"Yeah?" He rubbed at his crumpled T-shirt

again, looking around. "Well, tangling with vampires is obviously a great warm-up exercise."

"What'd you guys do? Lower your heads and run at each other from opposite sides of the yard?" asked Meredith.

"Something like that. He says he's going to watch Vickie now."

"Do you think we can trust him?" Meredith said soberly.

Matt considered. "As a matter of fact, I do. It's weird, but I don't think he's going to hurt her. And if the killer comes along, I think he's in for a surprise. Damon's spoiling for a fight. We might as well go back to the library for Stefan."

Stefan wasn't visible outside the library, but when the car had cruised up and down the street once or twice he materialized out of the darkness. He had a thick book with him.

"Breaking and entering and grand theft, library book," Meredith remarked. "I wonder what you get for that these days?"

"I borrowed it," Stefan said, looking aggrieved. "That's what libraries are for, right? And I copied what I needed out of the journal."

"You mean you found it? You figured it out? Then you can tell us everything, like you promised," Bonnie said. "Let's go to the boarding house."

Stefan looked slightly surprised when he

heard that Damon had turned up and stationed himself at Vickie's, but he made no comment. Matt didn't tell him exactly *how* Damon had turned up, and he noticed Bonnie didn't either.

"I'm almost positive about what's going on in Fell's Church. And I've got half the puzzle solved, anyway," Stefan said once they were all settled in his room in the boarding house attic. "But there's only one way to prove it, and only one way to solve the other half. I need help, but it isn't something I'm going to ask lightly." He was looking at Bonnie and Meredith as he said it.

They looked at each other, then back at him. "This guy killed one of our friends," said Meredith. "And he's driving another one crazy. If you need our help, you've got it."

"Whatever it takes," Bonnie added.

"It's something dangerous, isn't it?" Matt demanded. He couldn't restrain himself. As if Bonnie hadn't been through enough . . .

"It's dangerous, yes. But it's their fight too, you know."

"Darn right it is," said Bonnie. Meredith was obviously trying to repress a smile. Finally she had to turn away and grin.

"Matt's back," she said when Stefan asked her what the joke was.

"We missed you," added Bonnie. Matt

couldn't understand why they were all smiling at him, and it made him feel hot and uncomfortable. He went over to stand by the window.

"It *is* dangerous; I won't try to kid you about that," Stefan said to the girls. "But it's the only chance. The whole thing's a little complicated, and I'd better start at the beginning. We have to go back to the founding of Fell's Church . . ."

He talked on late into the night.

Thursday, June 11, 7:00 a.m.
Dear Diary,

I couldn't write last night, because I got in too late. Mom was upset again. She'd have been hysterical if she'd known what I was actually doing. Hanging out with vampires and planning something that may get me killed. That may get us all killed.

Stefan has a plan to trap the guy who murdered Sue. It reminds me of some of Elena's plans—and that's what worries me. They always sounded wonderful, but lots of the time they went wrong.

We talked about who gets the most dangerous job and decided it should be Meredith. Which is fine with me—I mean, she is stronger and more athletic, and she always keeps calm in emergencies. But it bugs me just a little that everybody was so quick *about choosing her, especially Matt. I mean, it's not like I'm totally incompetent. I know I'm not as smart as the others, and I'm certainly not as good at sports or as cool under pressure, but I'm not a total dweeb. I'm good for* something.

Anyway, we're going to do it after graduation. We're all in on it except Damon, who'll be watching Vickie. It's strange, but we all trust him now. Even me. Despite what he did to me last night, I don't think he'll let Vickie get hurt.

I haven't had any more dreams about Elena. I think if I do, I will go absolutely screaming berserk. Or never go to sleep again. I just can't take any more of that.

All right. I'd better go. Hopefully, by Sunday we'll have the mystery solved and the killer caught. I trust Stefan.

I just hope I can remember my part.

Nine

". . . And so, ladies and gentlemen, I give you the class of '92!"

Bonnie threw her cap into the air along with everyone else. We made it, she thought. Whatever happens tonight, Matt and Meredith and I made it to graduation. There had been times this last school year when she had seriously doubted they would.

Considering Sue's death, Bonnie had expected the graduation ceremony to be listless or grim. Instead, there was a sort of frenzied excitement about it. As if everyone was celebrating being alive—before it was too late.

It turned into rowdiness as parents surged forward and the senior class of Robert E. Lee fragmented in all directions, whooping and acting up. Bonnie retrieved her cap and then looked up into her mother's camera lens.

Act normal, that's what's important, she told herself. She caught a glimpse of Elena's aunt Judith and Robert Maxwell, the man Aunt Judith had recently married, standing on the sidelines. Robert was holding Elena's little sister, Margaret, by the hand. When they saw her, they smiled bravely, but she felt uncomfortable when they came her way.

"Oh, Miss Gilbert—I mean, Mrs. Maxwell—you shouldn't have," she said as Aunt Judith handed her a small bouquet of pink roses.

Aunt Judith smiled through the tears in her eyes. "This would have been a very special day for Elena," she said. "I want it to be special for you and Meredith, too."

"Oh, Aunt Judith." Impulsively, Bonnie threw her arms around the older woman. "I'm so sorry," she whispered. "You know how much."

"We all miss her," Aunt Judith said. Then she pulled back and smiled again and the three of them left. Bonnie turned from looking at them with a lump in her throat to look at the madly celebrating crowd.

There was Ray Hernandez, the boy she'd gone to Homecoming with, inviting everybody to a party at his house that night. There was Tyler's friend Dick Carter, making a fool of himself as usual. Tyler was smiling brazenly as his father took picture after picture. Matt was listening, with an unimpressed look, to some football recruiter from James Mason University. Meredith was standing nearby, holding a bouquet of red roses and looking pensive.

Vickie wasn't there. Her parents had kept her home, saying she was in no state to go out. Caroline wasn't there either. She was staying in the apartment in Heron. Her mother had told Bonnie's mother she had the flu, but Bonnie knew the truth. Caroline was scared.

And maybe she's right, Bonnie thought, moving toward Meredith. Caroline may be the only one of us to make it through next week.

Look normal, act normal. She reached Meredith's group. Meredith was wrapping the red-and-black tassel from her cap around the bouquet, twisting it between elegant, nervous fingers.

Bonnie threw a quick glance around. Good. This was the place. And now was the time.

"Be careful with that; you'll ruin it," she said aloud.

Meredith's look of thoughtful melancholy didn't change. She went on staring at the tassel, kinking it up. "It doesn't seem fair," she said, "that we should get these and Elena shouldn't. It's wrong."

"I know; it's awful," Bonnie said. But she kept her tone light. "I wish there was something we could do about it, but we can't."

"It's all *wrong*," Meredith went on, as if she hadn't heard. "Here we are out in the sunlight, graduating, and there she is under that—stone."

"I know, I know," Bonnie said in a soothing tone. "Meredith, you're getting yourself all upset. Why don't you try to think about something else? Look, after you go out to dinner with your parents, do you want to go to Raymond's party? Even if we're not invited, we can crash it."

"No!" Meredith said with startling vehemence. "I don't want to go to any party. How can you even think of that, Bonnie? How can you be so shallow?"

"Well, we've got to do *something* . . ."

"I'll tell you what *I'm* doing. I'm going up to the cemetery after dinner. I'm going to put *this* on Elena's grave. She's the one who deserves it." Meredith's knuckles were white as she shook the tassel in her hand.

"Meredith, don't be an idiot. You can't go up there, especially at night. That's crazy. Matt would say the same thing."

"Well, I'm not asking Matt. I'm not asking anybody. I'm going by myself."

"You can't. God, Meredith, I always thought you had some brains—"

"And I always thought you had some sensitivity. But obviously you don't even want to think about Elena. Or is it just because you want her old boyfriend for yourself?"

Bonnie slapped her.

It was a good hard slap, with plenty of energy behind it. Meredith drew in a sharp breath, one hand to her reddening cheek. Everyone around them was staring.

"That's it for you, Bonnie McCullough," Meredith said after a moment, in a voice of deadly quiet. "I don't ever want to speak to you again." She turned on her heel and walked away.

"Never would be too soon for me!" Bonnie shouted at her retreating back.

Eyes were hastily averted as Bonnie looked around her. But there was no question that she and Meredith had been the center of attention for several minutes past. Bonnie bit the inside of her cheek to keep a straight face and walked over to Matt, who had lost the recruiter.

"How was that?" she murmured.

"Good."

"Do you think the slap was too much? We didn't really plan that; I was just sort of going with the moment. Maybe it was too obvious . . ."

"It was fine, just fine." Matt was looking preoccupied. Not that dull, apathetic, turned-in look of the last few months, but distinctly abstracted.

"What is it? Something wrong with the plan?" Bonnie said.

"No, no. Listen, Bonnie, I've been thinking. You were the one to discover Mr. Tanner's body in the Haunted House last Halloween, right?"

Bonnie was startled. She gave an involuntary shiver of distaste. "Well, I was the first one to know he was dead, really dead, instead of just playing his scene. Why on earth do you want to talk about that now?"

"Because maybe you can answer this question. Could Mr. Tanner have got a knife in Damon?"

"What?"

"Well, could he?"

"I . . ." Bonnie blinked and frowned. Then she shrugged. "I suppose so. Sure. It was a Druid sacrifice scene, remember, and the knife we used was a real knife. We talked about using a fake one, but since Mr. Tanner was going to be lying right there beside it, we figured it was safe enough. As a matter of fact . . ." Bonnie's frown deepened. "I think when I found the body, the knife was in a different place from where we'd set it in the beginning. But then, some kid could have moved it. Matt, why are you asking?"

"Just something Damon said to me," Matt

said, staring off into the distance again. "I wondered if it could be the truth."

"Oh." Bonnie waited for him to say more, but he didn't. "Well," she said finally, "if it's all cleared up, can you come back to Earth, please? And don't you think you should maybe put your arm around me? Just to show you're on my side and there's no chance *you're* going to show up at Elena's grave tonight with Meredith?"

Matt snorted, but the faraway look disappeared from his eyes. For just a brief instant he put his arm around her and squeezed.

Déjà vu, Meredith thought as she stood at the gate to the cemetery. The problem was, she couldn't remember exactly which of her previous experiences in the graveyard this night reminded her of. There had been so many.

In a way, it had all started here. It had been here that Elena had sworn not to rest until Stefan belonged to her. She'd made Bonnie and Meredith swear to help her, too—in blood. How suitable, Meredith thought now.

And it had been here that Tyler had assaulted Elena the night of the Homecoming dance. Stefan had come to the rescue, and that had been the beginning for them. This graveyard had seen a lot.

It had even seen the whole group of them file

up the hill to the ruined church last December, looking for Katherine's lair. Seven of them had gone down into the crypt: Meredith herself, Bonnie, Matt, and Elena, with Stefan, Damon, and Alaric. But only six of them had come out all right. When they took Elena out of there, it was to bury her.

This graveyard had been the beginning, and the end as well. And maybe there would be another end tonight.

Meredith started walking.

I wish you were here now, Alaric, she thought. I could use your optimism and your savvy about the supernatural—and I wouldn't mind your muscles, either.

Elena's headstone was in the new cemetery, of course, where the grass was still tended and the graves marked with wreaths of flowers. The stone was very simple, almost plain looking, with a brief inscription. Meredith bent down and placed her bouquet of roses in front of it. Then, slowly, she added the red-and-black tassel from her cap. In this dim light, both colors looked the same, like dried blood. She knelt and folded her hands quietly. And she waited.

All around her the cemetery was still. It seemed to be waiting with her, breath held in anticipation. The rows of white stones stretched on either side of her, shining faintly. Meredith listened for any sound.

And then she heard one. Heavy footsteps.

With her head down, she stayed quiet, pretending she noticed nothing.

The footsteps sounded closer, not even bothering to be stealthy.

"Hi, Meredith."

Meredith looked around quickly. "Oh—Tyler," she said. "You scared me. I thought you were—never mind."

"Yeah?" Tyler's lips skinned back in an unsettling grin. "Well, I'm sorry you're disappointed. But it's me, just me and nobody else."

"What are you doing here, Tyler? No good parties?"

"I could ask you the same question." Tyler's eyes dropped to the headstone and the tassel and his face darkened. "But I guess I already know the answer. You're here for *her*. Elena Gilbert, A Light in Darkness," he read sarcastically.

"That's right," Meredith said evenly. " 'Elena' means light, you know. And she was certainly surrounded by darkness. It almost beat her, but she won in the end."

"Maybe," Tyler said, and worked his jaw meditatively, squinting. "But you know, Meredith, it's a funny thing about darkness. There's always more of it waiting in the wings."

"Like tonight," Meredith said, looking up at the sky. It was clear and dotted with faint stars. "It's very dark tonight, Tyler. But sooner or later the sun will come up."

"Yeah, but the moon comes up first." Tyler chuckled suddenly, as if at some joke only he could see. "Hey, Meredith, you ever see the Smallwood family plot? Well, come on and I'll show you. It's not far."

Just like he showed Elena, Meredith thought. In a way she was enjoying this verbal fencing, but she never lost sight of what she had come here for. Her cold fingers dipped into her jacket pocket and found the tiny sprig of vervain there. "That's all right, Tyler. I think I'd prefer to stay here."

"You sure about that? A cemetery's a dangerous place to be alone."

Unquiet spirits, Meredith thought. She looked right at him. "I know."

He was grinning again, displaying teeth like tombstones. "Anyway, you can see it from here if you have good eyes. Look that way, toward the old graveyard. Now, do you see something sort of shining red in the middle?"

"No." There was a pale luminosity over the trees in the east. Meredith kept her eyes on it.

"Aw, come on, Meredith. You're not trying. Once the moon's up you'll see it better."

"Tyler, I can't waste any more time here. I'm going."

"No, you're not," he said. And then, as her fingers tightened on the vervain, encompassing it in her fist, he added in a wheedling voice, "I mean, you're not going until I tell you the story of that headstone, are you? It's a great story. See, the headstone is made of red marble, the only one of its kind in the whole graveyard. And that ball on top—see it?—that must weigh about a ton. But it moves. It turns whenever a Smallwood is going to die. My grandfather didn't believe that; he put a scratch on it right down the front. He used to come out and check it every month or so. Then one day he came and found the scratch in the rear. The ball had turned completely backward. He did everything he could to turn it around, but he couldn't. It was too heavy. And that night, in bed, he died. They buried him under it."

"He probably had a heart attack from overexertion," Meredith said caustically, but her palms were tingling.

"You're funny, aren't you? Always so cool. Always so together. Takes a lot to make you scream, doesn't it?"

"I'm leaving, Tyler. I've had enough."

He let her walk a few paces, then said, "You

screamed that night at Caroline's, though, didn't you?"

Meredith turned back. "How do you know that?"

Tyler rolled his eyes. "Give me credit for a little intelligence, okay? I know a lot, Meredith. For instance, I know what's in your pocket."

Meredith's fingers stilled. "What do you mean?"

"Vervain, Meredith. *Verbena officinalis*. I've got a friend who's into these things." Tyler was focused now, his smile growing, watching her face as if it were his favorite TV show. Like a cat tired of playing with a mouse, he was moving in. "And I know what it's for, too." He cast an exaggerated glance around and put a finger to his lips. "Shh. Vampires," he whispered. Then he threw back his head and laughed loudly.

Meredith backed away a step.

"You think that's going to help you, don't you? But I'm going to tell you a secret."

Meredith's eyes measured the distance between herself and the path. She kept her face calm, but a violent shaking was beginning inside her. She didn't know if she was going to be able to pull this off.

"You're not going anywhere, babe," Tyler said, and a large hand clasped Meredith's wrist. It was hot and damp where she could feel it below her jacket cuff. "You're going to stay right here for your surprise." His body was hunched now, his head thrust forward, and there was an exultant leer on his lips.

"Let me go, Tyler. You're hurting me!" Panic flashed down all Meredith's nerves at the feel of Tyler's flesh against hers. But the hand only gripped harder, grinding tendon against bone in her wrist.

"This is a secret, baby, that nobody else knows," Tyler said, pulling her close, his breath hot in her face. "You came here all decked out against vampires. But I'm not a vampire."

Meredith's heart was pounding. "Let *go*!"

"First I want you to look over there. You can see the headstone now," he said, turning her so that she couldn't help but look. And he was right; she *could* see it, like a red monument with a shining globe on top. Or—not a globe. That marble ball looked like . . . it looked like . . .

"Now look east. What do you see there, Meredith?" Tyler went on, his voice hoarse with excitement.

It was the full moon. It had risen while he'd been talking to her, and now it hung above the hills, perfectly round and enormously distended, a huge and swollen red ball.

And that was what the headstone looked like. Like a full moon dripping with blood.

"You came here protected against vampires, Meredith," Tyler said from behind her, even more hoarsely. "But the Smallwoods aren't vampires at all. We're something else."

And then he growled.

No human throat could have made the sound. It wasn't an imitation of an animal; it was *real*. A vicious guttural snarl that went up and up, snapping Meredith's head around to look at him, to stare in disbelief. What she was seeing was so horrible her mind couldn't accept it . . .

Meredith screamed.

"I told you it was a surprise. How do you like it?" Tyler said. His voice was thick with saliva, and his red tongue lolled among the rows of long canine teeth. His face wasn't a face anymore. It jutted out grotesquely into a muzzle, and his eyes were yellow, with slitlike pupils. His reddish-sandy hair had grown over his cheeks and down the back of his neck. A pelt. "You can scream all you want up here and nobody's going to hear you," he added.

Every muscle in Meredith's body was rigid, trying to get away from him. It was a visceral reaction, one she couldn't have helped if she wanted to. His breath was so hot, and it smelled feral, like an animal. The nails he was digging into her wrist were stumpy blackened claws. She didn't have the strength to scream again.

"There's other things besides vampires with a taste for blood," Tyler said in his new slurping voice. "And I want to taste yours. But first we're going to have some fun."

Although he still stood on two feet, his body was humped and strangely distorted. Meredith's struggles were feeble as he forced her to the ground. She was a strong girl, but he was far stronger, his muscles bunching under his shirt as he pinned her.

"You've always been too good for me, haven't you? Well, now you're going to find out what you've been missing."

I can't breathe, Meredith thought wildly. His arm was across her throat, blocking her air. Gray waves rolled through her brain. If she passed out now . . .

"You're going to wish you died as fast as Sue." Tyler's face floated above her, red as the moon, with that long tongue lolling. His other hand held her arms above her head. "You ever hear the story of Little Red Riding Hood?"

The gray was turning into blackness, speckled with little lights. Like stars, Meredith thought. I'm falling in the stars . . .

"Tyler, take your hands off her! Let go of her, now!" Matt's voice shouted.

Tyler's slavering snarl broke off into a surprised whine. The arm against Meredith's throat released pressure, and air rushed into her lungs.

Footsteps were pounding around her. "I've been waiting a long time to do this, Tyler," Matt said, jerking the sandy-red head back by the hair. Then Matt's fist smashed into Tyler's newly grown muzzle. Blood spurted from the wet animal nose.

The sound Tyler made froze Meredith's heart in her chest. He sprang at Matt, twisting in midair, claws outstretched. Matt fell back under the assault and Meredith, dizzy, tried to push herself up off the ground. She couldn't; all her muscles were trembling uncontrollably. But someone else picked Tyler off Matt as if Tyler weighed no more than a doll.

"Just like old times, Tyler," Stefan said, setting Tyler on his feet and facing him.

Tyler stared a minute, then tried to run.

He was fast, dodging with animal agility between the rows of graves. But Stefan was faster and cut him off.

"Meredith, are you hurt? Meredith?" Bonnie was kneeling beside her. Meredith nodded—she still couldn't speak—and let Bonnie support her head. "I knew we should have stopped him sooner, I knew it," Bonnie went on worriedly.

Stefan was dragging Tyler back. "I always knew you were a jerk," he said, shoving Tyler against a headstone, "but I didn't know you were this stupid. I'd have thought you would have learned not to jump girls in graveyards, but no. And you had to brag about what you did to Sue, too. That wasn't smart, Tyler."

Meredith looked at them as they faced each other. So different, she thought. Even though they were both creatures of darkness in some way. Stefan was pale, his green eyes blazing with anger and menace, but there was a dignity, almost a purity about him. He was like some stern angel carved in unyielding marble. Tyler just looked like a trapped animal. He was crouched, breathing hard, blood and saliva mingling on his chest. Those yellow eyes glittered with hate and fear, and his fingers worked as if he'd like to claw something. A low sound came out of his throat.

"Don't worry, I'm not going to beat you up this time," Stefan said. "Not unless you try to get away. We're all going up to the church to have a little chat. You like to tell stories, Tyler; well, you're going to tell me one now."

Tyler sprang at him, vaulting straight from the ground for Stefan's throat. But Stefan was ready for him. Meredith suspected that both Stefan and Matt enjoyed the next few minutes, working off their accumulated aggressions, but she didn't, so she looked away.

In the end, Tyler was trussed up with nylon

cord. He could walk, or shuffle at least, and Stefan held the back of his shirt and guided him ungently up the path to the church.

Inside, Stefan pushed Tyler onto the ground near the open tomb. "Now," he said, "we are going to talk. And you're going to cooperate, Tyler, or you're going to be very, very sorry."

Ten

Meredith sat down on the knee-high wall of the ruined church. "You said it was going to be dangerous, Stefan, but you didn't say you were going to let him strangle me."

"I'm sorry. I was hoping he'd give some more information, especially after he admitted to being there when Sue died. But I shouldn't have waited."

"I haven't admitted anything! You can't prove anything," Tyler said. The animal whine was back in his voice, but on the walk up his face and body had returned to normal. Or rather, they'd returned to human, Meredith thought. The swelling and bruises and dried blood weren't normal.

"This isn't a court of law, Tyler," she said. "Your father can't help you now."

"But if it were, we'd have a pretty good case," Stefan added. "Enough to put you away on conspiracy to commit murder, I think."

"That's if somebody doesn't melt down their grandma's teaspoons to make a silver bullet," Matt put in.

Tyler looked from one to another of them. "I won't tell you anything."

"Tyler, you know what you are? You're a bully," Bonnie said. "And bullies always talk."

"You don't mind pinning a girl down and threatening her," said Matt, "but when her friends turn up, you're scared spitless."

Tyler just glared at all of them.

"Well, if you don't want to talk, I guess *I'll* have to," Stefan said. He leaned down and picked up the thick book he'd gotten from the library. One foot on the lip of the tomb, he rested the book on his knee and opened it. In that moment, Meredith thought, he looked frighteningly like Damon.

"This is a book by Gervase of Tilbury, Tyler," he said. "It was written around the year 1210 A.D. One of the things it talks about is werewolves."

"You can't prove anything! You don't have any evidence—"

"Shut up, Tyler!" Stefan looked at him. "I don't need to prove it. I can *see* it, even now.

Have you forgotten what I am?" There was a silence, and then Stefan went on. "When I got here a few days ago, there was a mystery. A girl was dead. But who killed her? And why? All the clues I could see seemed contradictory.

"It wasn't an ordinary killing, not some human psycho off the street. I had the word of somebody I trusted on that—and independent evidence, too. An ordinary killer can't work a Ouija board by telekinesis. An ordinary killer can't cause fuses to blow in a power plant hundreds of miles away.

"No, this was somebody with tremendous physical and psychic power. From everything Vickie told me, it sounded like a vampire.

"Except that Sue Carson still had her blood. A vampire would have drained at least some of it. No vampire could resist that, especially not a killer. That's where the high comes from, and the high's the reason to kill. But the police doctor found no holes in her veins, and only a small amount of bleeding. It didn't make sense.

"And there was another thing. *You* were in that house, Tyler. You made the mistake of grabbing Bonnie that night, and then you made the mistake of shooting off your mouth the next day, saying things you couldn't have known unless you were there.

"So what did we have? A seasoned vampire, a

vicious killer with Power to spare? Or a high school bully who couldn't organize a trip to the toilet without falling over his own feet? Which? The evidence pointed both ways, and I couldn't make up my mind.

"Then I went to see Sue's body myself. And there it was, the biggest mystery of all. A cut *here*." Stefan's finger sketched a sharp line down from his collarbone. "Typical, traditional cut—made by vampires to share their own blood. But Sue *wasn't* a vampire, and she didn't make that cut herself. Someone made it for her as she lay there dying on the ground."

Meredith shut her eyes, and she heard Bonnie swallow hard beside her. She put out a hand and found Bonnie's and held tight, but she went on listening. Stefan had not gone into this kind of detail in his explanation to them before.

"Vampires don't need to cut their victims like that; they use their teeth," Stefan said. His upper lip lifted slightly to show his own teeth. "But if a vampire wanted to draw blood *for somebody else to drink*, he might cut instead of biting. If a vampire wanted to give someone else the first and only taste, he might do that.

"And *that* started me thinking about blood. Blood is important, you see. For vampires, it gives life, Power. It's all we need for survival, and there are times when needing it drives us crazy. But it's good for other things, too. For instance . . . initiation.

"Initiation and Power. Now I was thinking about those two things, putting them together with what I'd seen of *you*, Tyler, when I was in Fell's Church before. Little things I hadn't really focused on. But I remembered something Elena had told me about your family history, and I decided to check it out in Honoria Fell's journal."

Stefan lifted a piece of paper from between the pages of the book he held. "And there it was, in Honoria's handwriting. I Xeroxed the page so I could read it to you. The Smallwoods' little family secret—if you can read between the lines."

Looking down at the paper, he read:

"*November 12. Candles made, flax spun. We are short on cornmeal and salt, but we will get through the winter. Last night an alarm; wolves attacked Jacob Smallwood as he returned from the forest. I treated the wound with whortleberry and sallow bark, but it is deep and I am afraid. After coming home I cast the runes. I have told no one but Thomas the results.*

"Casting the runes is divining," Stefan added, looking up. "Honoria was what we'd call a witch. She goes on here to talk about 'wolf trouble' in various other parts of the settlement—it seems that all of a sudden there were frequent attacks, especially on young girls. She tells how she and her husband became more and more concerned. And finally, this:

"*December 20. Wolf trouble at the Smallwoods' again. We heard the screams a few minutes ago, and Thomas said it was time. He made the bullets yesterday. He has loaded his rifle and we will walk over. If we are spared, I will write again.*

"*December 21. Went over to Smallwoods' last night. Jacob sorely afflicted. Wolf killed.*

"*We will bury Jacob in the little graveyard at the foot of the hill. May his soul find peace in death.*

"In the official history of Fell's Church," Stefan said, "that's been interpreted to mean that Thomas Fell and his wife went over to the Smallwoods' to find Jacob Smallwood being attacked by a wolf again, and that the wolf killed him. But that's wrong. What it really says is *not* that the wolf killed Jacob Smallwood but that Jacob Smallwood, *the wolf*, was killed."

Stefan shut the book. "He was a werewolf, your great - great - great - whatever grandfather, Tyler. He got that way by being attacked by a werewolf himself. And he passed his werewolf virus on to the son who was born eight and a half months after he died. Just the way your father passed it on to you."

"I always knew there was something about you, Tyler," Bonnie said, and Meredith opened her eyes. "I never could tell what it was, but at the back of my mind something was telling me you were creepy."

"We used to make jokes about it," Meredith said, her voice still husky. "About your 'animal magnetism' and your big white teeth. We just never knew how close to the mark we were."

"Sometimes psychics can sense that kind of thing," Stefan conceded. "Sometimes even ordinary people can. *I* should have seen it, but I was preoccupied. Still, that's no excuse. And obviously somebody else—the psychic killer—saw it right away. Didn't he, Tyler? A man wearing an old raincoat came to you. He was tall, with blond hair and blue eyes, and he made some kind of a deal with you. In exchange for—*something*—he'd show you how to reclaim your heritage. How to become a real werewolf.

"Because according to Gervase of Tilbury"—Stefan tapped the book on his knee—"a werewolf who hasn't been bitten himself needs to be initiated. That means you can have the werewolf virus all your life but never even know it because it's never activated. Generations of Smallwoods have lived and died, but the virus was dormant in them because they didn't know the secret of waking it up. But the man in the raincoat knew. He knew that you have to kill and taste fresh blood. After that, at the first full moon you can change." Stefan glanced up, and Meredith followed his gaze to the white disk of the moon in the sky. It looked clean and two dimensional now, no longer a sullen red globe.

A look of suspicion passed over Tyler's fleshy features, and then a look of renewed fury. "You tricked me! You planned this!"

"Very clever," said Meredith, and Matt said, "No kidding." Bonnie wet her finger and marked an imaginary 1 on an invisible scoreboard.

"I knew you wouldn't be able to resist following one of the girls here if you thought she'd be alone," said Stefan. "You'd think that the graveyard was the perfect place to kill; you'd have complete privacy. And I knew you wouldn't be able to resist bragging about what you'd done. I was hoping you'd tell Meredith more about the other killer, the one who actually threw Sue out the window, the one who cut her so you could drink fresh blood. The vampire, Tyler. Who is he? Where is he hiding?"

Tyler's look of venomous hatred changed to a sneer. "You think I'd tell you that? He's my friend."

"He is not your friend, Tyler. He's using you. And he's a murderer."

"Don't get in any deeper, Tyler," Matt added.

"You're already an accessory. Tonight you tried to kill Meredith. Pretty soon you're not going to be able to go back even if you want to. Be smart and stop this now. Tell us what you know."

Tyler bared his teeth. "I'm not telling you *anything*. How're you going to make me?"

The others exchanged glances. The atmosphere changed, became charged with tension as they all turned back to Tyler.

"You really don't understand, do you?" Meredith said quietly. "Tyler, you helped *kill* Sue. She died for an obscene ritual so that you could change into that *thing* I saw. You were planning to kill me, and Vickie and Bonnie too, I'm sure. Do you think we have any pity for you? Do you think we brought you up here to be nice to you?"

There was a silence. The sneer was fading from Tyler's lips. He looked from one face to another.

They were all implacable. Even Bonnie's small face was unforgiving.

"Gervase of Tilbury mentions one interesting thing," Stefan said, almost pleasantly. "There's a cure for werewolves besides the traditional silver bullet. Listen." By moonlight, he read from the book on his knee. "*It is commonly reported and held by grave and worthy doctors that if a werewolf be shorn of one of his members, he shall surely re-*

cover his original body. Gervase goes on to tell the story of Raimbaud of Auvergne, a werewolf who was cured when a carpenter cut off one of his hind paws. Of course, that was probably hideously painful, but the story goes that Raimbaud thanked the carpenter 'for ridding him forever of the accursed and damnable form.' " Stefan raised his head. "Now, I'm thinking that if Tyler won't help us with information, the least we can do is make sure he doesn't go out and kill again. What do the rest of you say?"

Matt spoke up. "I think it's our duty to cure him."

"All we have to do is relieve him of one of his members," Bonnie agreed.

"I can think of one right off," Meredith said under her breath.

Tyler's eyes were starting to bulge. Under the dirt and blood his normally ruddy face had gone pale. "You're bluffing!"

"Get the ax, Matt," said Stefan. "Meredith, you take off one of his shoes."

Tyler kicked when she did, aiming for her face. Matt came and got his head in a hammerlock. "Don't make it any worse on yourself, Tyler."

The bare foot Meredith exposed was big, the sole as sweaty as Tyler's palms. Coarse hair sprouted from the toes. It made Meredith's skin crawl.

"Let's get this over with," she said.

"You're joking!" Tyler howled, thrashing so that Bonnie had to come and grab his other leg and kneel on it. "You can't do this! You can't!"

"Keep him still," Stefan said. Working together, they stretched Tyler out, his head locked in Matt's arm, his legs spread and pinned by the girls. Making sure Tyler could see what he was doing, Stefan balanced a branch perhaps two inches thick on the lip of the tomb. He raised the ax and then brought it down hard, severing the stick with one blow.

"It's sharp enough," he said. "Meredith, roll his pants leg up. Then tie some of that cord just above his ankle as tight as you can for a tourniquet. Otherwise he'll bleed out."

"You can't do this!" Tyler was screaming. "*You can't doooooo this!*"

"Scream all you want, Tyler. Up here, nobody's going to hear you, right?" Stefan said.

"You're no better than I am!" Tyler yelled in a spray of spittle. "You're a killer too!"

"I know exactly what I am," Stefan said. "Believe me, Tyler. I know. Is everybody ready? Good. Hold on to him; he's going to jump when I do it."

Tyler's screams weren't even words anymore.

Matt was holding him so that he could see Stefan kneel and take aim, hefting the ax blade above Tyler's ankle to gauge force and distance.

"Now," said Stefan, raising the ax high.

"*No! No!* I'll talk to you! I'll talk!" shrieked Tyler.

Stefan glanced at him. "Too late," he said, and brought the ax down.

It rebounded off the stone floor with a clang and a spark, but the noise was drowned by Tyler's screaming. It seemed to take Tyler several minutes to realize that the blade hadn't touched his foot. He paused for breath only when he choked, and turned wild, bulging eyes on Stefan.

"Start talking," Stefan said, his voice wintry, remorseless.

Little whimpers were coming from Tyler's throat and there was foam on his lips. "I don't know his name," he gasped out. "But he looks like you said. And you're right; he's a vampire, man! I saw him drain a ten-point buck while it was still kicking. He *lied* to me," Tyler added, the whine creeping back into his voice. "He told me I'd be stronger than anybody, as strong as him. He said I could have any girl I wanted, any way I wanted. The creep lied."

"He told you that you could kill and get away with it," Stefan said.

"He said I could do Caroline that night. She

had it coming after the way she ditched me. I wanted to make her beg—but she got out of the house somehow. I could have Caroline and Vickie, he said. All he wanted was Bonnie and Meredith."

"But you just tried to kill Meredith."

"That was *now*. Things are different now, stupid. He said it was all right."

"Why?" Meredith asked Stefan in an undertone.

"Maybe because you'd served your purpose," he said. "You'd brought me here." Then he went on, "All right, Tyler, show us you're cooperating. Tell us how we can get this guy."

"*Get* him? You're nuts!" Tyler burst into ugly laughter, and Matt tightened the arm around his throat. "Hey, choke me all you want; it's still the truth. He told me he's one of the Old Ones, one of the Originals, whatever that means. He said he's been making vampires since before the pyramids. He said he's made a bargain with the devil. You could stick a stake in his heart and it wouldn't do *anything*. You can't kill him." The laughter became uncontrolled.

"Where's he hiding, Tyler?" Stefan rapped out. "Every vampire needs a place to sleep. Where is it?"

"He'd kill me if I told you that. He'd *eat* me,

man. God, if I told you what he did to that buck before it died . . ." Tyler's laughter was turning into something like sobs.

"Then you'd better help us destroy him before he can find you, hadn't you? What's his weak point? How's he vulnerable?"

"God, that poor buck . . ." Tyler was blubbering.

"What about Sue? Did you cry over *her*?" Stefan said sharply. He picked up the ax. "I think," he said, "that you're wasting our time."

The ax lifted.

"No! No! I'll talk to you; I'll tell you something. Look, there's one kind of wood that can hurt him—not kill him, but hurt him. He admitted that but didn't tell me what it was! I swear to you that's the truth!"

"Not good enough, Tyler," said Stefan.

"For God's sake—I'll tell you where he's going tonight. If you get over there fast enough, maybe you can stop him."

"What do you mean, where he's going tonight? Talk fast, Tyler!"

"He's going to Vickie's, okay? He said tonight we get one each. That's helpful, isn't it? If you hurry, maybe you can get there!"

Stefan had frozen, and Meredith felt her heart racing. Vickie. They hadn't even thought about an attack on Vickie.

"Damon's guarding her," Matt said. "Right, Stefan? Right?"

"He's supposed to be," Stefan said. "I left him there at dusk. If something happened, he should have called me . . ."

"You guys," Bonnie whispered. Her eyes were big and her lips were trembling. "I think we'd better get over there *now*."

They stared at her a moment and then everyone was moving. The ax clanged on the floor as Stefan dropped it.

"Hey, you can't leave me like this! I can't drive! He's gonna come back for me! Come back and untie my hands!" Tyler shrieked. None of them answered.

They ran all the way down the hill and piled into Meredith's car. Meredith took off speeding, rounding corners dangerously fast and gliding through stop signs, but there was a part of her that didn't want to get to Vickie's house. That wanted to turn around and drive the other way.

I'm calm; I'm the one who's always calm, she thought. But that was on the outside. Meredith knew very well how calm you could look on the outside when inside everything was breaking up.

They rounded the last corner onto Birch Street and Meredith hit the brakes.

"Oh, God!" Bonnie cried from the backseat. "No! No!"

"Quick," Stefan said. "There may still be a chance." He wrenched open the door and was out even before the car had stopped. But in back, Bonnie was sobbing.

Eleven

The car skidded in behind one of the police cars that was parked crookedly in the street. There were lights everywhere, lights flashing blue and red and amber, lights blazing from the Bennett house.

"Stay here," Matt snapped, and he plunged outside, following Stefan.

"No!" Bonnie's head jerked up; she wanted to grab him and drag him back. The dizzy nausea she'd felt ever since Tyler had mentioned Vickie was overwhelming her. It was too late; she'd known in the first instant that it was too late. Matt was only going to get himself killed too.

"You stay, Bonnie—keep the doors locked. I'll go after them." That was Meredith.

"No! I'm sick of having everybody tell me to *stay*!" Bonnie cried, struggling with the seat belt, finally getting it unlocked. She was still crying, but she could see well enough to get out of the car and start toward Vickie's house. She heard Meredith right behind her.

The activity all seemed concentrated at the front: people shouting, a woman screaming, the crackling voices of police radios. Bonnie and Meredith headed straight for the back, for Vickie's window. What is wrong with this picture? Bonnie thought wildly as they approached. The wrongness of what she was looking at was undeniable, yet hard to put a finger on. Vickie's window was open—but it *couldn't* be open; the middle pane of a bay window never opens, Bonnie thought. But then how could the curtains be fluttering out like shirttails?

Not open, broken. Glass was all over the gravel pathway, grinding underfoot. There were shards like grinning teeth left in the bare frame. Vickie's house had been broken into.

"She asked him *in*," Bonnie cried in agonized fury. "Why did she *do* that? Why?"

"Stay here," Meredith said, trying to moisten dry lips.

"*Stop telling me that.* I can take it, Meredith. I'm *mad*, that's all. I *hate* him." She gripped Meredith's arm and went forward.

The gaping hole got closer and closer. The

curtains rippled. There was enough space between them to see inside.

At the last moment, Meredith pushed Bonnie away and looked through first herself. It didn't matter. Bonnie's psychic senses were awake and already telling her about this place. It was like the crater left in the ground after a meteor has hit and exploded, or like the charred skeleton of a forest after a wildfire. Power and violence were still thrumming in the air, but the main event was over. This place had been violated.

Meredith spun away from the window, doubling over, retching. Clenching her fists so that the nails bit into her palms, Bonnie leaned forward and looked in.

The smell was what struck her first. A wet smell, meaty and coppery. She could almost taste it, and it tasted like an accidentally bitten tongue. The stereo was playing something she couldn't hear over the screaming out front and the drumming-surf sound in her own ears. Her eyes, adjusting from the darkness outside, could see only red. Just red.

Because that was the new color of Vickie's room. The powder blue was gone. Red wallpaper, red comforter. Red in great gaudy splashes across the floor. As if some kid had gotten a bucket of red paint and gone crazy.

The record player clicked and the stylus

swung back to the beginning. With a shock, Bonnie recognized the song as it started over.

It was "Goodnight Sweetheart."

"You monster," Bonnie gasped. Pain shot through her stomach. Her hand gripped the window frame, tighter, tighter. "You monster, I *hate* you! I hate you!"

Meredith heard and straightened up, turning. She shakily pushed back her hair and managed a few deep breaths, trying to look as if she could cope. "You're cutting your hand," she said. "Here, let me see it."

Bonnie hadn't even realized she was gripping broken glass. She let Meredith take the hand, but instead of letting her examine it, she turned it over and clasped Meredith's own cold hand tightly. Meredith looked terrible: dark eyes glazed, lips blue-white and shaking. But Meredith was still trying to take care of her, still trying to keep it together.

"Go on," she said, looking at her friend intently. "Cry, Meredith. Scream if you want to. But get it out somehow. You don't have to be cool now and keep it all inside. You have every right to lose it today."

For a moment Meredith just stood there, trembling, but then she shook her head with a ghastly attempt at a smile. "I can't. I'm just not made that way. Come on, let me look at the hand."

Bonnie might have argued, but just then Matt came around the corner. He started violently to see the girls standing there.

"What are you doing—?" he began. Then he saw the window.

"She's dead," Meredith said flatly.

"I know." Matt looked like a bad photograph of himself, an overexposed one. "They told me up front. They're bringing out . . ." He stopped.

"We blew it. Even after we promised her . . ." Meredith stopped too. There was nothing more to say.

"But the police will have to believe us now," Bonnie said, looking at Matt, then Meredith, finding one thing to be grateful for. "They'll *have* to."

"No," Matt said, "they won't, Bonnie. Because they're saying it's a suicide."

"A *suicide*? Have they seen that room? They call *that* a suicide?" Bonnie cried, her voice rising.

"They're saying she was mentally unbalanced. They're saying she—got hold of some scissors . . ."

"Oh, my God," Meredith said, turning away.

"They think maybe she was feeling guilty for having killed Sue."

"Somebody broke into this house," Bonnie said fiercely. "They've got to admit that!"

"No." Meredith's voice was soft, as if she were very tired. "Look at the window here. The glass is all outside. Somebody from the inside broke it." And that's the rest of what's wrong with the picture, Bonnie thought.

"*He* probably did, getting out," Matt said. They looked at each other silently, in defeat.

"Where's Stefan?" Meredith asked Matt quietly. "Is he out front where everyone can see him?"

"No, once we found out she was dead he headed back this way. I was coming to look for him. He must be around somewhere . . ."

"Sh!" said Bonnie. The shouting from the front had stopped. So had the woman's screaming. In the relative stillness they could hear a faint voice from beyond the black walnut trees in the back of the yard.

"—while *you* were supposed to be watching her!"

The tone made Bonnie's skin break out in gooseflesh. "That's him!" Matt said. "And he's with Damon. Come on!"

Once they were among the trees Bonnie could

hear Stefan's voice clearly. The two brothers were facing each other in the moonlight.

"I trusted you, Damon. I trusted you!" Stefan was saying. Bonnie had never seen him so angry, not even with Tyler in the graveyard. But it was more than anger.

"And you just let it happen," Stefan went on, without glancing at Bonnie and the others as they appeared, without giving Damon a chance to reply. "Why didn't you do *something*? If you were too much of a coward to fight him, you could at least have called for me. But you just stood there!"

Damon's face was hard, closed. His black eyes glittered, and there was nothing lazy or casual about his posture now. He looked as unbending and brittle as a pane of glass. He opened his mouth, but Stefan interrupted.

"It's my own fault. I should have known better. I *did* know better. *They* all knew, they warned me, but I wouldn't listen."

"Oh, did *they*?" Damon snapped a glance toward Bonnie on the sidelines. A chill went through her.

"Stefan, wait," Matt said. "I think—"

"I should have listened!" Stefan was raging on. He didn't even seem to hear Matt. "I should have stayed with her myself. I promised her she would be safe—and I lied! She died thinking I betrayed her." Bonnie could see it in his face now, the guilt eating into him like acid. "If I had stayed here—"

"You would be dead too!" Damon hissed. "This isn't an ordinary vampire you're dealing with. He would have broken you in two like a dry twig—"

"*And that would have been better!*" Stefan cried. His chest was heaving. "I would rather have died with her than stood by and watched it! What happened, Damon?" He had gotten hold of himself now, and he was calm, too calm; his green eyes were burning feverishly in his pale face, his voice vicious, poisonous, as he spoke. "Were you too busy chasing some other girl through the bushes? Or just too uninterested to interfere?"

Damon said nothing. He was just as pale as his brother, every muscle tense and rigid. Waves of black fury were rising from him as he watched Stefan.

"Or maybe you enjoyed it," Stefan was continuing, moving another half step forward so that he was right in Damon's face. "Yes, that was probably it; you liked it, being with another killer. Was it good, Damon? Did he let you watch?"

Damon's fist jerked back and he hit Stefan.

It happened too fast for Bonnie's eye to follow. Stefan fell backward onto the soft ground, long legs sprawling. Meredith cried out something, and Matt jumped in front of Damon.

Brave, Bonnie thought dazedly, but stupid. The air was crackling with electricity. Stefan raised a hand to his mouth and found blood, black in the moonlight. Bonnie lurched over to his side and grabbed his arm.

Damon was coming after him again. Matt fell back before him, but not all the way. He dropped to his knees beside Stefan, sitting on his heels, one hand upraised.

"Enough, you guys! Enough, all right?" he shouted.

Stefan was trying to get up. Bonnie held on to his arm more firmly. "No! Stefan, don't! Don't!" she begged. Meredith grabbed his other arm.

"Damon, leave it alone! Just leave it!" Matt was saying sharply.

We're all crazy, getting in the middle of this, Bonnie thought. Trying to break up a fight between two angry vampires. They're going to kill us just to shut us up. Damon's going to swat Matt like a fly.

But Damon had stopped, with Matt blocking his way. For a long moment the scene remained frozen, nobody moving, everybody rigid with strain. Then, slowly, Damon's stance relaxed.

His hands lowered and unclenched. He drew a

slow breath. Bonnie realized she'd been holding her own breath, and she let it out.

Damon's face was cold as a statue carved in ice. "All right, have it your way," he said, and his voice was cold too. "But I'm through here. I'm leaving. And this time, *brother*, if you follow me, I'll kill you. Promise or no promise."

"I won't follow you," Stefan said from where he sat. His voice sounded as if he'd been swallowing ground glass.

Damon hitched up his jacket, straightening it. With a glance at Bonnie that scarcely seemed to see her, he turned to go. Then he turned back and spoke clearly and precisely, each word an arrow aimed at Stefan.

"I warned you," he said. "About what I am, and about which side would win. You should have listened to *me*, little brother. Maybe you'll learn something from tonight."

"I've learned what trusting you is worth," Stefan said. "Get out of here, Damon. I never want to see you again."

Without another word, Damon turned and walked away into the darkness.

Bonnie let go of Stefan's arm and put her head in her hands.

Stefan got up, shaking himself like a cat that had been held against its will. He walked a little distance from the others, his face averted from them. Then he simply stood there. The rage seemed to have left him as quickly as it had come.

What do we say now? Bonnie wondered, looking up. What *can* we say? Stefan was right about one thing: they had warned him about Damon and he hadn't listened. He'd truly seemed to believe that his brother could be trusted. And then they'd all gotten careless, relying on Damon because it was easy and because they needed the help. No one had argued against letting Damon watch Vickie tonight.

They were all to blame. But it was Stefan who would tear himself apart with guilt over this. She knew that was behind his out-of-control fury at Damon: his own shame and remorse. She wondered if Damon knew that, or cared. And she wondered what had really happened tonight. Now that Damon had left, they would probably never know.

No matter what, she thought, it was better he was gone.

Outside noises were reasserting themselves: cars being started in the street, the short burst of a siren, doors slamming. They were safe in the little grove of trees for the moment, but they couldn't stay here.

Meredith had one hand pressed to her forehead, her eyes shut. Bonnie looked from her to

Stefan, to the lights of Vickie's silent home beyond the trees. A wave of sheer exhaustion passed through her body. All the adrenaline that had been supporting her throughout this evening seemed to have drained away. She didn't even feel angry anymore at Vickie's death; only depressed and sick and very, very tired. She wished she could crawl into her bed at home and pull the blankets over her head.

"Tyler," she said aloud. And when they all turned to look at her, she said, "We left him in the ruined church. And he's our last hope now. We've got to make him help us."

That roused everyone. Stefan turned around silently, not speaking and not meeting anyone's eyes as he followed them back to the street. The police cars and ambulance were gone, and they drove to the cemetery without incident.

But when they reached the ruined church, Tyler wasn't there.

"We left his feet untied," Matt said heavily, with a grimace of self-disgust. "He must have walked away since his car's still down there." Or he could have been taken, Bonnie thought. There was no mark on the stone floor to show which.

Meredith went to the knee-high wall and sat down, one hand pinching the bridge of her nose.

Bonnie sagged against the belfry.

They'd failed completely. That was the long and short of it tonight. They'd lost and *he* had won. Everything they'd done today had ended in defeat.

And Stefan, she could tell, was taking the whole responsibility on his own shoulders.

She glanced at the dark, bowed head in the front seat as they drove back to the boarding house. Another thought occurred to her, one that sent thrills of alarm down her nerves. Stefan was all they had to protect them now that Damon was gone. And if Stefan himself was weak and exhausted . . .

Bonnie bit her lip as Meredith pulled up to the barn. An idea was forming in her mind. It made her uneasy, even frightened, but another look at Stefan put steel in her resolve.

The Ferrari was still parked behind the barn—apparently Damon had abandoned it. Bonnie wondered how he planned to get about the countryside, and then thought of wings. Velvety soft, strong black crow's wings that reflected rainbows in their feathers. Damon didn't need a car.

They went into the boarding house just long enough for Bonnie to call her parents and say she was spending the night at Meredith's. This was her idea. But after Stefan had climbed the stairs to his attic room, Bonnie stopped Matt on the front porch.

"Matt? Can I ask you a favor?"

He swung around, blue eyes widening. "That's a loaded phrase. Every time Elena said those particular words . . ."

"No, no, this is nothing terrible. I just want you to take care of Meredith, see she's okay once she gets home and all." She gestured toward the other girl, who was already walking toward the car.

"But you're coming with us."

Bonnie glanced at the stairs through the open door. "No. I think I'll stay a few minutes. Stefan can drive me home. I just want to talk to him about something."

Matt looked bewildered. "Talk to him about what?"

"Just something. I can't explain now. Will you, Matt?"

"But . . . oh, all right. I'm too tired to care. Do what you want. I'll see you tomorrow." He walked off, seeming baffled and a little angry.

Bonnie was baffled herself at his attitude. Why *should* he care, tired or not, if she talked to Stefan? But there was no time to waste puzzling over it. She faced the stairs and, squaring her shoulders, went up them.

The bulb in the attic ceiling lamp was missing, and Stefan had lighted a candle. He was lying haphazardly on the bed, one leg off and one leg on, his eyes shut. Maybe asleep. Bonnie tiptoed up and fortified herself with a deep breath.

"Stefan?"

His eyes opened. "I thought you'd left."

"They did. I didn't." God, he's pale, thought Bonnie. Impulsively, she plunged right in.

"Stefan, I've been thinking. With Damon gone, you're the only thing between us and the killer. That means you've got to be strong, as strong as you can be. And, well, it occurred to me that maybe . . . you know . . . you might need . . ." Her voice faltered. Unconsciously she'd begun fiddling with the wad of tissues forming a makeshift bandage on her palm. It was still bleeding sluggishly from where she'd cut it on the glass.

His gaze followed hers down to it. Then his eyes lifted quickly to her face, reading the confirmation there. There was a long moment of silence.

Then he shook his head.

"But why? Stefan, I don't want to get personal, but frankly you don't look so good. You're not going to be much help to anybody if you collapse on us. And . . . I don't mind, if you only take a little. I mean, I'm never going to miss it, right? And it can't hurt all that much. And . . ." Once again her voice trailed off. He was just looking at her, which was very disconcerting. "Well, why *not?*" she demanded, feeling slightly let down.

"Because," he said softly, "I made a promise. Maybe not in so many words, but—a promise just the same. I won't take human blood as food, because that means *using* a person, like livestock. And I won't exchange it with anyone, because that means love, and—" This time he was the one who couldn't finish. But Bonnie understood.

"There won't ever be anyone else, will there?" she said.

"No. Not for me." Stefan was so tired that his control was slipping and Bonnie could see behind the mask. And again she saw that pain and need, so great that she had to look away from him.

A strange little chill of premonition and dismay trickled through her heart. Before, she had wondered if Matt would ever get over Elena, and he had, it seemed. But Stefan—

Stefan, she realized, the chill deepening, was different. No matter how much time passed, no matter what he did, he would never truly heal. Without Elena he would always be half himself, only half alive.

She had to think of something, do something,

to push this awful feeling of dread away. Stefan needed Elena; he couldn't be whole without her. Tonight he'd started to crack up, swinging between dangerously tight control and violent rage. If only he could see Elena for just a minute and talk to her . . .

She'd come up here to give Stefan a gift that he didn't want. But there was something else he did want, she realized, and only she had the power to give it to him.

Without looking at him, her voice husky, she said, "Would you like to see Elena?"

Dead silence from the bed. Bonnie sat, watching the shadows in the room sway and flicker. At last, she chanced a look at him out of the corner of her eye.

He was breathing hard, eyes shut, body taut as a bowstring. Trying, Bonnie diagnosed, to work up the strength to resist temptation.

And losing. Bonnie saw that.

Elena always had been too much for him.

When his eyes met hers again, they were grim, and his mouth was a tight line. His skin wasn't pale anymore but flushed with color. His body was still trembling-taut and keyed up with anticipation.

"You might get hurt, Bonnie."

"I know."

"You'd be opening yourself up to forces beyond your control. I can't guarantee that I can protect you from them."

"I know. How do you want to do it?"

Fiercely, he took her hand. "Thank you, Bonnie," he whispered.

She felt the blood rise to her face. "That's all right," she said. Good *grief*, he was gorgeous. Those eyes . . . in a minute she was either going to jump him or melt into a puddle on his bed. With a pleasurably agonizing feeling of virtue she removed her hand from his and turned to the candle.

"How about if I go into a trance and try to reach her, and then, once I make contact, try to find you and draw you in? Do you think that would work?"

"It might, if I'm reaching for you too," he said, withdrawing that intensity from her and focusing it on the candle. "I can touch your mind . . . when you're ready, I'll feel it."

"Right." The candle was white, its wax sides smooth and shining. The flame drew itself up and then fell back. Bonnie stared until she became lost in it, until the rest of the room blacked out around her. There was only the flame, herself and the flame. She was going into the flame.

Unbearable brightness surrounded her. Then she passed through it into the dark.

* * *

The funeral home was cold. Bonnie glanced around uneasily, wondering how she had gotten here, trying to gather her thoughts. She was all alone, and for some reason that bothered her. Wasn't somebody else supposed to be here too? She was looking for someone.

There was light in the next room. Bonnie moved toward it and her heart began pounding. It was a visitation room, and it was filled with tall candelabras, the white candles glimmering and quivering. In the midst of them was a white coffin with an open lid.

Step by step, as if something were pulling her, Bonnie approached the casket. She didn't want to look in. She had to. There was something in that coffin waiting for her.

The whole room was suffused with the soft white light of the candles. It was like floating in an island of radiance. But she didn't want to look . . .

Moving as if in slow motion, she reached the coffin, stared at the white satin lining inside. It was empty.

Bonnie closed it and leaned against it, sighing.

Then she caught motion in her peripheral vision and whirled.

It was Elena.

"Oh, God, you scared me," Bonnie said.

"I thought I told you not to come here," Elena answered.

This time her hair was loose, flowing over her shoulders and down her back, the pale golden white of a flame. She was wearing a thin white dress that glowed softly in the candlelight. She looked like a candle herself, luminous, radiant. Her feet were bare.

"I came here to . . ." Bonnie floundered, some concept teasing around the edges of her mind. This was *her* dream, her trance. She had to remember. "I came here to let you see Stefan," she said.

Elena's eyes widened, her lips parting. Bonnie recognized the look of yearning, of almost irresistible longing. Not fifteen minutes ago she'd seen it on Stefan's face.

"Oh," Elena whispered. She swallowed, her eyes clouding. "Oh, Bonnie . . . but I *can't*."

"Why not?"

Tears were shining in Elena's eyes now, and her lips were trembling. "What if things start to change? What if *he* comes, and . . ." She put a hand to her mouth and Bonnie remembered the last dream, with teeth falling like rain. Bonnie met Elena's eyes with understanding horror.

"Don't you see? I couldn't stand it if something like that happened," Elena whispered. "If he saw me like that . . . And I can't control things here; I'm not strong enough. Bonnie, please don't let him through. Tell him how sorry I am. Tell him—" She shut her eyes, tears spilling.

"All right." Bonnie felt as if she might cry too, but Elena was right. She reached for Stefan's mind to explain to him, to help him bear the disappointment. But the instant she touched it she knew she'd made a mistake.

"Stefan, no! Elena says—" It didn't matter. His mind was stronger than hers, and the instant she'd made contact he had taken over. He'd sensed the gist of her conversation with Elena, but he wasn't going to take no for an answer. Helplessly, Bonnie felt herself being overridden, felt his mind come closer, closer to the circle of light formed by the candelabras. She felt his presence there, felt it taking shape. She turned and saw him, dark hair, tense face, green eyes fierce as a falcon's. And then, knowing there was nothing more she could do, she stepped back to allow them to be alone.

Twelve

Stefan heard a voice whisper, soft with pain, "Oh, no."

A voice that he'd never thought to hear again, that he would never forget. Ripples of chills poured over his skin, and he could feel a shaking start inside him. He turned toward the voice, his attention fixing instantly, his mind almost shutting down because it couldn't cope with so many sudden driving emotions at once.

His eyes were blurred and could only discern a wash of radiance like a thousand candles. But it didn't matter. He could *feel* her there. The same presence he had sensed the very first day he'd come to Fell's Church, a golden white light that shone into his consciousness. Full of cool beauty and searing passion and vibrant life. Demanding that he move toward it, that he forget everything else.

Elena. It was really Elena.

Her presence pervaded him, filling him to his fingertips. All his hungry senses were fixed on that wash of luminance, searching for her. Needing her.

Then she stepped out.

She moved slowly, hesitantly. As if she could barely make herself do it. Stefan was caught in the same paralysis.

Elena.

He saw her every feature as if for the first time. The pale gold hair floating about her face and shoulders like a halo. The fair, flawless skin. The slender, supple body just now canted away from him, one hand raised in protest.

"Stefan," the whisper came, and it was *her* voice. Her voice saying his name. But there was such pain in it that he wanted to run to her, hold her, promise her that everything would be all right. "Stefan, please . . . I *can't* . . ."

He could see her eyes now. The dark blue of lapis lazuli, flecked in this light with gold. Wide with pain and wet with unshed tears. It shredded his guts.

"You don't want to see me?" His voice was dry as dust.

"I don't want *you* to see *me*. Oh, Stefan, he

can make anything happen. And he'll find us. He'll come here . . ."

Relief and aching joy flooded through Stefan. He could scarcely concentrate on her words, and it didn't matter. The way she said his name was enough. That "Oh, Stefan" told him everything he cared about.

He moved toward her quietly, his own hand coming up to reach for hers. He saw the protesting shake of her head, saw that her lips were parted with her quickening breath. Up close, her skin had an inner glow, like a flame shining through translucent candle wax. Droplets of wetness were caught on her eyelashes like diamonds.

Although she kept shaking her head, kept protesting, she did not move her hand away. Not even when his outspread fingers touched it, pressing against her cool fingertips as if they were on opposite sides of a pane of glass.

And at this distance her eyes could not evade his. They were looking at each other, looking and not turning aside. Until at last she stopped whispering "Stefan, no" and only whispered his name.

He couldn't think. His heart was threatening to come through his chest. Nothing mattered except that she was here, that they were here together. He didn't notice the strange surroundings, didn't care who might be watching.

Slowly, so slowly, he closed his hand around hers, intertwining their fingers, the way they were meant to be. His other hand lifted to her face.

Her eyes closed at the touch, her cheek leaning into it. He felt the moisture on his fingers and a laugh caught in his throat. Dream tears. But they were real, *she* was real. Elena.

Sweetness pierced him. A pleasure so sharp it was a pain, just to stroke the tears away from her face with his thumb.

All the frustrated tenderness of the last six months, all the emotion he'd kept locked in his heart that long, came cascading out, submerging him. Drowning both of them. It took such a little movement and then he was holding her.

An angel in his arms, cool and thrilling with life and beauty. A being of flame and air. She shivered in his embrace; then, eyes still shut, put up her lips.

There was nothing cool about the kiss. It struck sparks from Stefan's nerves, melting and dissolving everything around it. He felt his control unraveling, the control he'd worked so hard to preserve since he'd lost her. Everything inside him was being jarred loose, all knots untied, all floodgates opened. He could feel his own tears as he held her to him, trying to fuse them into one flesh, one body. So that nothing could ever separate them again.

They were both crying without breaking the kiss. Elena's slender arms were around his neck now, every inch of her fitting to him as if she had never belonged anywhere else. He could taste the salt of her tears on his lips and it drenched him with sweetness.

He knew, vaguely, that there was something else he should be thinking about. But the first electric touch of her cool skin had driven reason from his mind. They were in the center of a whirlwind of fire; the universe could explode or crumble or burn to ashes for all he cared, as long as he could keep her safe.

But Elena was trembling.

Not just from emotion, from the intensity that was making him dizzy and drunk with pleasure. From fear. He could feel it in her mind and he wanted to protect her, to shield her and to cherish her and to *kill* anything that dared frighten her. With something like a snarl he raised his face to look around.

"What is it?" he said, hearing the predator's rasp in his own voice. "Anything that tries to hurt you—"

"Nothing can hurt me." She still clung to him, but she leaned back to look into his face. "I'm afraid for *you*, Stefan, for what he might do to you. And for what he might make you see . . ." Her voice quavered. "Oh, Stefan, go now, before he comes. He can find you through me. Please, please, go . . ."

"Ask me anything else and I'll do it," Stefan said. The killer would have to shred him nerve from nerve, muscle from muscle, cell from cell to make him leave her.

"Stefan, it's only a dream," Elena said desperately, new tears falling. "We can't really touch, we can't be together. It's not allowed."

Stefan didn't care. It didn't seem like a dream. It felt real. And even in a dream he was not going to give up Elena, not for anyone. No force in heaven or hell could make him . . .

"Wrong, sport. Surprise!" said a new voice, a voice Stefan had never heard. He recognized it instinctively, though, as the voice of a killer. A hunter among hunters. And when he turned, he remembered what Vickie, poor Vickie, had said.

He looks like the devil.

If the devil was handsome and blond.

He wore a threadbare raincoat, as Vickie had described. Dirty and tattered. He looked like any street person from any big city, except that he was so tall and his eyes were so clear and penetrating. Electric blue, like razor-frosted sky. His hair was almost white, standing straight up as if blown by a blast of chilly wind. His wide smile made Stefan feel sick.

"Salvatore, I presume," he said, scraping a bow. "And of course the beautiful Elena. The beautiful *dead* Elena. Come to join her, Stefan? You two were just meant to be together."

He looked young, older than Stefan, but still young. He wasn't.

"Stefan, leave now," Elena whispered. "He can't hurt me, but you're different. He can make something happen that will follow you out of the dream."

Stefan's arm stayed locked around her.

"Bravo!" the man in the raincoat applauded, looking around as if to encourage an invisible audience. He staggered slightly, and if he'd been human, Stefan would have thought he was drunk.

"Stefan, *please*," Elena whispered.

"It would be rude to leave before we've even been properly introduced," the blond man said. Hands in coat pockets, he strode a step or two closer. "Don't you want to know who I am?"

Elena shook her head, not in negation but in defeat, and dropped it to Stefan's shoulder. He cupped a hand around her hair, wanting to shield every part of her from this madman.

"I want to know," he said, looking at the blond man over her head.

"I don't see why you didn't ask me in the first place," the man replied, scratching his cheek with his middle finger. "Instead of going to everybody else. *I'm* the only one who can tell you. I've been around a long time."

"How long?" said Stefan, unimpressed.

"A *long* time . . ." The blond man's gaze turned dreamy, as if looking back over the years. "I was tearing pretty white throats when your ancestors were building the Colosseum. I killed with Alexander's army. I fought in the Trojan War. I'm old, Salvatore. I'm one of the Originals. In my earliest memories I carried a bronze ax."

Slowly, Stefan nodded.

He'd heard of the Old Ones. They were whispered about among vampires, but no one Stefan had ever known had actually met one. Every vampire was made by another vampire, changed by the exchange of blood. But somewhere, back in time, had been the Originals, the ones who *hadn't* been made. They were where the line of continuity stopped. No one knew how they'd gotten to be vampires themselves. But their Powers were legendary.

"I helped bring the Roman Empire down," the blond man continued dreamily. "They called us barbarians—they just didn't understand! War, Salvatore! There's nothing like it. Europe was exciting then. I decided to stick around the countryside and enjoy myself. Strange, you know, people never really seemed comfortable around me. They used to run or hold up crosses." He shook his head. "But one woman came and asked my help. She was a maid in a baron's household, and her little mistress was sick. Dying, she said. She wanted me to do something about it. And so . . ." The smile returned and broadened, getting wider and impossibly wider, "I did. She was a pretty little thing."

Stefan had turned his body to hold Elena away from the blond man, and now, for a moment, he turned his head away too. He should have known, should have guessed. And so it all came back to him. Vickie's death, and Sue's, were ultimately to be laid at his door. He had started the chain of events that ended here.

"Katherine," he said, lifting his head to look at the man. "You're the vampire who changed Katherine."

"To *save* her *life*," the blond man said, as if Stefan were stupid at learning a lesson. "Which your little sweetheart here took."

A name. Stefan was searching for a name in his mind, knowing that Katherine had told it to him, just as she must have described this man to him once. He could hear Katherine's words in his mind: *I woke in the middle of the night and I saw the man that Gudren, my maid, had brought. I was frightened. His name was Klaus and I'd heard the people in the village say he was evil . . .*

"Klaus," the blond man said mildly, as if agreeing with something. "That was what *she* called me, anyway. She came back to me after two little Italian boys jilted her. She'd done everything for them, changed them into vampires, given them eternal life, but they were ungrateful and threw her out. Very strange."

"That isn't how it happened," Stefan said through his teeth.

"What was even stranger was that she never got over you, Salvatore. You especially. She was always drawing unflattering comparisons between us. I tried to beat some sense into her, but it never really worked. Maybe I should have just killed her myself, I don't know. But by then I'd gotten used to having her around. She never was the brightest. But she was good to look at, and she knew how to have fun. I showed her that, how to enjoy the killing. Eventually her brain turned a little, but so what? It wasn't her brains I was keeping her for."

There was no longer any vestige of love for Katherine in Stefan's heart, but he found he could still hate the man who had made her what she was in the end.

"Me? *Me*, sport?" Klaus pointed to his own chest in unbelief. "*You* made Katherine into what she is right now, or rather your little girlfriend did. *Right now*, she's dust. Worm's meat. But your sweetie is just slightly beyond my reach at present. Vibrating on a higher plane, isn't that what the mystics say, Elena? Why don't you vibrate down here with the rest of us?"

"If only I could," whispered Elena, lifting her head and looking at him with hatred.

"Oh, well. Meanwhile I've got your friends. Sue was such a *sweet* girl, I hear." He licked his lips. "And Vickie was delectable. Delicate but full bodied, with a nice bouquet. More like a nineteen-year-old than seventeen."

Stefan lunged one step forward, but Elena caught him. "Stefan, don't! This is his territory, and his mental powers are stronger than ours. He controls it."

"Precisely. This is my territory. Unreality." Klaus grinned his staring psychotic grin again. "Where your wildest nightmares come true, free of charge. For instance," he said, looking at Stefan, "how'd you like to see what your sweetheart really looks like right now? Without her makeup?"

Elena made a soft sound, almost a moan. Stefan held her tighter.

"It's been how long since she died? About six months? Do you know what happens to a body once it's been in the ground six months?" Klaus licked his lips again, like a dog.

Now Stefan understood. Elena shivered, head bent, and tried to move away from him, but he locked his arms around her.

"It's all right," he said to her softly. And to Klaus: "You're forgetting yourself. I'm not a human who jumps at shadows and the sight of blood. I know about death, Klaus. It doesn't frighten me."

"No, but does it thrill you?" Klaus's voice dropped, low, intoxicating. "Isn't it exciting, the stench, the rot, the fluids of decomposing flesh? Isn't it a *kick*?"

"Stefan, let me go. *Please*." Elena was shaking, pushing at him with her hands, all the time keeping her head twisted away so he couldn't see her face. Her voice sounded close to tears. "*Please*."

"The only Power you have here is the power of illusion," Stefan said to Klaus. He held Elena to him, cheek pressed to her hair. He could feel the changes in the body he embraced. The hair under his cheek seemed to coarsen and Elena's form to shrink on itself.

"In certain soils the skin can tan like leather," Klaus assured him, bright eyed, grinning.

"Stefan, I don't want you to look at me—"

Eyes on Klaus, Stefan gently pushed the coarsened white hair away and stroked the side of Elena's face, ignoring the roughness against his fingertips.

"But of course most of the time it just decomposes. What a way to go. You lose everything, skin, flesh, muscles, internal organs—all back into the ground. . . ."

The body in Stefan's arms was dwindling. He shut his eyes and held tighter, hatred for Klaus burning inside him. An illusion, it was all an illusion . . .

"Stefan . . ." It was a dry whisper, faint as the scratch of paper blown down a sidewalk. It hung on the air a minute and then vanished, and Stefan found himself holding a pile of bones.

"And finally it ends up like that, in over two hundred separate, easy-to-assemble pieces. Comes with its own handy-dandy carrying case. . . ." On the far side of the circle of light there was a creaking sound. The white coffin there was opening by itself, the lid lifting. "Why don't you do the honors, Salvatore? Go put Elena where she belongs."

Stefan had dropped to his knees, shaking, looking at the slender white bones in his hands. It was all an illusion—Klaus was merely controlling Bonnie's trance and showing Stefan what he wanted Stefan to see. He hadn't really hurt Elena, but the hot, protective fury inside Stefan wouldn't recognize that. Carefully, Stefan laid the fragile bones on the ground and touched them once, gently. Then he looked up at Klaus, lips curled with contempt.

"*That* is not Elena," he said.

"Of course it is. I'd recognize her anywhere." Klaus spread his hands and declaimed, " '*I knew a woman, lovely in her bones* . . .' "

"No." Sweat was beading on Stefan's forehead. He shut out Klaus's voice and concentrated, fists clenched, muscles cracking with effort. It was like pushing a boulder uphill, fighting Klaus's influence. But where they lay, the delicate bones began trembling, and a faint golden light shone around them.

" '*A rag and a bone and a hank of hair* . . . *the fool he called them his lady fair* . . .' "

The light was shimmering, dancing, linking the bones together. Warm and golden it folded about them, clothing them as they rose in the air. What stood there now was a featureless form of soft radiance. Sweat ran into Stefan's eyes and he felt as if his lungs would burst.

" '*Clay lies still, but blood's a rover* . . .' "

Elena's hair, long and silky gold, arranged itself over glowing shoulders. Elena's features, blurred at first and then clearly focused, formed on the face. Lovingly, Stefan reconstructed every detail. Thick lashes, small nose, parted lips like rose petals. White light swirled around the figure, creating a thin gown.

" '*And the crack in the teacup opens a lane to the land of the dead . . .*' "

"No." Dizziness swept over Stefan as he felt the last surge of Power sigh out of him. A breath lifted the figure's breast, and eyes blue as lapis lazuli opened.

Elena smiled, and he felt the blaze of her love arc to meet him. "Stefan." Her head was high, proud as any queen's.

Stefan turned to Klaus, who had stopped speaking and was glaring mutely.

"This," Stefan said distinctly, "is Elena. Not whatever empty shell she's left behind in the ground. This is Elena, and nothing you do can ever touch her."

He held out his hand, and Elena took it and stepped to him. When they touched, he felt a jolt, and then felt her Powers flowing into him, sustaining him. They stood together, side by side, facing the blond man. Stefan had never felt as fiercely victorious in his life, or as strong.

Klaus stared at them for perhaps twenty seconds and then went berserk.

His face twisted in loathing. Stefan could feel waves of malignant Power battering against him and Elena, and he used all his strength to resist it. The maelstrom of dark fury was trying to tear them apart, howling through the room, destroying everything in its path. Candles snuffed out and flew into the air as if caught in a tornado. The dream was breaking up around them, shattering.

Stefan clung to Elena's other hand. The wind blew her hair, whipping it around her face.

"Stefan!" She was shouting, trying to make herself heard. Then he heard her voice in his mind. "*Stefan, listen to me! There is one thing you can do to stop him. You need a victim, Stefan—find one of his victims. Only a victim will know—*"

The noise level was unbearable, as if the very fabric of space and time was tearing. Stefan felt Elena's hands ripped from his. With a cry of desperation, he reached out for her again, but he could feel nothing. He was already drained by the effort of fighting Klaus, and he couldn't hold on to consciousness. The darkness took him spinning down with it.

Bonnie had seen everything.

It was strange, but once she stepped aside to let Stefan go to Elena, she seemed to lose physical presence in the dream. It was as if she were no longer a player but the stage the action was being played upon. She could watch, but she couldn't do anything else.

In the end, she'd been afraid. She wasn't strong enough to hold the dream together, and the whole thing finally exploded, throwing her out of the trance, back into Stefan's room.

He was lying on the floor and he looked dead. So white, so still. But when Bonnie tugged at him, trying to get him on the bed, his chest heaved and she heard him suck in a gasping breath.

"Stefan? Are you okay?"

He looked wildly around the room as if trying to find something. "Elena!" he said, and then he stopped, memory clearly returning.

His face twisted. For one dreadful instant Bonnie thought he was going to cry, but he only shut his eyes and dropped his head into his hands.

"Stefan?"

"I lost her. I couldn't hold on."

"I know." Bonnie watched him a moment, then, gathering her courage, knelt in front of him, touching his shoulders. "I'm sorry."

His head lifted abruptly, his green eyes dry but so dilated they looked black. His nostrils were flared, his lips drawn back from his teeth.

"Klaus!" He spat the name as if it were a curse. "Did you see him?"

"Yes," Bonnie said, pulling back. She gulped,

her stomach churning. "He's crazy, isn't he, Stefan?"

"Yes." Stefan got up. "And he must be stopped."

"But how?" Since seeing Klaus, Bonnie was more frightened than ever, more frightened and less confident. "What could stop him, Stefan? I've never felt anything like that Power."

"But didn't you—?" Stefan turned to her quickly. "Bonnie, didn't you hear what Elena said at the end?"

"No. What do you mean? I couldn't hear anything; there was a slight hurricane going on at the time."

"Bonnie . . ." Stefan's eyes went distant with speculation and he spoke as if to himself. "That means that *he* probably didn't hear it either. So he doesn't know, and he won't try to stop us."

"From what? Stefan, what are you talking about?"

"From finding a victim. Listen, Bonnie, Elena told me that if we can find a surviving victim of Klaus's, we can find a way to stop him."

Bonnie was in completely over her head. "But . . . why?"

"Because vampires and their donors—their prey—share minds briefly while the blood is being exchanged. Sometimes the donor can learn things about the vampire that way. Not always, but occasionally. That's what must have happened, and Elena knows it."

"That's all very well and good—except for one small thing," Bonnie said tartly. "Will you please tell me who on *earth* could have survived an attack by Klaus?"

She expected Stefan to be deflated, but he wasn't. "A vampire," he said simply. "A human Klaus made into a vampire would qualify as a victim. As long as they've exchanged blood, they've touched minds."

"Oh. *Oh*. So . . . if we can find a vampire he's made . . . but *where*?"

"Maybe in Europe." Stefan began to pace around the room, his eyes narrowed. "Klaus has a long history, and some of his vampires are bound to be there. I may have to go and look for one."

Bonnie was utterly dismayed. "But Stefan, you can't leave *us*. You can't!"

Stefan stopped where he was, across the room, and stood very still. Then at last, he turned to face her. "I don't want to," he said quietly. "And we'll try to think of another solution first—maybe we can get hold of Tyler again. I'll wait a week, until next Saturday. But I may have to leave, Bonnie. You know that as well as I do."

There was a long, long silence between them.

Bonnie fought the heat in her eyes, determined to be grown up and mature. She wasn't a baby and she would prove that now, once and for all. She caught Stefan's gaze and slowly nodded.

Thirteen

June 19, Friday, 11:45 p.m.
Dear Diary,

Oh, God, what are we going to do?

This has been the longest week of my life. Today was the last day of school and tomorrow Stefan is leaving. He's going to Europe to search for a vampire who got changed by Klaus. He says he doesn't want to leave us unprotected. But he's going to go.

We can't find Tyler. His car disappeared from the cemetery, but he hasn't turned up at school. He's missed every final this week. Not that the rest of us are doing much better. I wish Robert E. Lee was like the schools that have all their finals before graduation. I don't know whether I'm writing English or Swahili these days.

I hate *Klaus. From what I saw he's as crazy as Katherine—and even crueler. What he did to Vickie*

—but I can't even talk about that or I'll start crying again. He was just playing with us at Caroline's party, like a cat with a mouse. And to do it on Meredith's birthday, too—although I suppose he couldn't have known that. He seems to know a lot, though. He doesn't talk like a foreigner, not like Stefan did when he first came to America, and he knows all about American things, even songs from the fifties. Maybe he's been over here for a while . . .

Bonnie stopped writing. She thought desperately. All this time, they had been thinking of victims in Europe, of vampires. But from the way Klaus talked, he had obviously been in America a long time. He didn't sound foreign at all. And he'd chosen to attack the girls on Meredith's birthday . . .

Bonnie got up, reached for the telephone, and called Meredith's number. A sleepy male voice answered.

"Mr. Sulez, this is Bonnie. Can I speak to Meredith?"

"Bonnie! Don't you know what time it is?"

"Yes." Bonnie thought quickly. "But it's about —about a final we had today. Please, I have to talk with her."

There was a long pause, then a heavy sigh. "Just a minute."

Bonnie tapped her fingers impatiently as she waited. At last there was the click of another phone being picked up.

"Bonnie?" came Meredith's voice. "What's wrong?"

"Nothing. I mean—" Bonnie was excruciatingly conscious of the open line, of the fact that Meredith's father hadn't hung up. He might be listening. "It's about—that German problem we've been working on. *You* remember. The one we couldn't figure out for the final. You know how we've been looking for the one person who can help us solve it? Well, I think I know who it is."

"You *do*?" Bonnie could sense Meredith scrambling for the right words. "Well—who is it? Does it involve any long-distance calls?"

"No," Bonnie said, "it doesn't. It hits a lot closer to home, Meredith. A lot. In fact, you could say it's right in your own backyard, hanging on your family tree."

The line was silent so long Bonnie wondered if Meredith was still there. "Meredith?"

"I'm thinking. Does this solution have anything to do with coincidence?"

"Nope." Bonnie relaxed and smiled slightly, grimly. Meredith had it now. "Not a thing to do with coincidence. It's more a case of history repeating itself. Deliberately repeating itself, if you see what I mean."

"Yes," Meredith said. She sounded as if she were recovering from a shock, and no wonder. "You know, I think you just may be right. But there's still the matter of persuading—this person—to actually help us."

"You think that may be a problem?"

"I think it could. Sometimes people get very rattled—about a test. Sometimes they even kind of lose their minds."

Bonnie's heart sank. This was something that hadn't occurred to her. What if he *couldn't* tell them? What if he were that far gone?

"All we can do is try," she said, making her voice as optimistic as possible. "Tomorrow we'll have to try."

"All right. I'll pick you up at noon. Good night, Bonnie."

"Night, Meredith." Bonnie added, "I'm sorry."

"No, I think it may be for the best. So that history doesn't continue to repeat itself forever. Good-bye."

Bonnie pressed the disconnect button on the handset, clicking it off. Then she just sat for a few minutes, her finger on the button, staring at the wall. Finally she replaced the handset in its cradle and picked up her diary again. She put a period on the last sentence and added a new one.

We are going to see Meredith's grandfather tomorrow.

"I'm an idiot," Stefan said in Meredith's car the next day. They were going to West Virginia, to the institution where Meredith's grandfather was a patient. It was going to be a fairly long drive.

"We're all idiots. Except Bonnie," Matt said. Even in the midst of her anxiety Bonnie felt a warm glow at that.

But Meredith was shaking her head, eyes on the road. "Stefan, you couldn't have realized, so stop beating up on yourself. You didn't know that Klaus attacked Caroline's party on the anniversary of the attack on my grandfather. And it didn't occur to Matt or me that Klaus could have been in America for so long because we never saw Klaus or heard him speak. We were thinking of people he could have attacked in Europe. Really, Bonnie was the only one who *could* have put it all together, because she had all the information."

Bonnie stuck out her tongue. Meredith caught it in the rearview mirror and arched an eyebrow. "Just don't want you getting too cocky," she said.

"I won't; modesty is one of my most charming qualities," Bonnie replied.

Matt snorted, but then he said, "I still think it was pretty smart," which started the glow all over again.

The institution was a terrible place. Bonnie tried as hard as she could to conceal her horror and disgust, but she knew Meredith could sense it. Meredith's shoulders were stiff with defensive pride as she walked down the halls in front of them. Bonnie, who had known her for so many years, could see the humiliation underneath that pride. Meredith's parents considered her grandfather's condition such a blot that they never allowed him to be mentioned to outsiders. It had been a shadow over the entire family.

And now Meredith was showing that secret to strangers for the first time. Bonnie felt a rush of love and admiration for her friend. It was so like Meredith to do it without fuss, with dignity, letting nobody see what it cost her. But the institution was still terrible.

It wasn't filthy or filled with raving maniacs or anything like that. The patients looked clean and well cared for. But there was something about the sterile hospital smells and the halls crowded with motionless wheelchairs and blank eyes that made Bonnie want to run.

It was like a building full of zombies. Bonnie saw one old woman, her pink scalp showing through thin white hair, slumped with her head on the table next to a naked plastic doll. When Bonnie reached out desperately, she found Matt's hand already reaching for hers. They followed Meredith that way, holding on so hard it hurt.

"This is his room."

Inside was another zombie, this one with white hair that still showed an occasional fleck of black like Meredith's. His face was a mass of wrinkles and lines, the eyes rheumy and rimmed with scarlet. They stared vacantly.

"Granddad," Meredith said, kneeling in front of his wheelchair, "Granddad, it's me, Meredith. I've come to visit you. I've got something important to ask you."

The old eyes never flickered.

"Sometimes he knows us," Meredith said quietly, without emotion. "But mostly these days he doesn't."

The old man just went on staring.

Stefan dropped to his heels. "Let me try," he said. Looking into the wrinkled face he began to speak, softly, soothingly, as he had to Vickie.

But the filmy dark eyes didn't so much as blink. They just went on staring aimlessly. The only movement was a slight, continuous tremor in the knotted hands on the arms of the wheelchair.

And no matter what Meredith or Stefan did, that was all the response they could elicit.

Eventually Bonnie tried, using her psychic powers. She could sense *something* in the old man, some spark of life trapped in the imprisoning flesh. But she couldn't reach it.

"I'm sorry," she said, sitting back and pushing hair out of her eyes. "It's no use. I can't do anything."

"Maybe we can come another time," Matt said, but Bonnie knew it wasn't true. Stefan was leaving tomorrow; there would never be another time. And it had seemed like such a good idea. . . . The glow that had warmed her earlier was ashes now, and her heart felt like a lump of lead. She turned away to see Stefan already starting out of the room.

Matt put a hand under her elbow to help her up and guide her out. And after standing for a minute with her head bent in discouragement, Bonnie let him. It was hard to summon up enough energy to put one foot in front of the other. She glanced back dully to see whether Meredith was following—

And *screamed*. Meredith was standing in the center of the room, facing the door, discouragement written on her face. But behind her, the figure in the wheelchair had stirred at last. In a silent explosion of movement, it had reared above her, the rheumy old eyes open wide and the mouth open wider. Meredith's grandfather looked as if he had been caught in the act of leaping—arms flung out, mouth forming a silent howl. Bonnie's screams rang from the rafters.

Everything happened at once then. Stefan came charging back in, Meredith spun around, Matt grabbed for her. But the old figure didn't leap. He stood towering above all of them, staring over their heads, seeming to see something none of them could. Sounds were coming from his mouth at last, sounds that formed one ululating word.

"*Vampire! Vampiiiire!*"

Attendants were in the room, crowding Bonnie and the others away, restraining the old man. Their shouts added to the pandemonium.

"*Vampire! Vampire!*" Meredith's grandfather caterwauled, as if warning the town. Bonnie felt panicked—was he looking at Stefan? Was it an accusation?

"Please, you'll have to leave now. I'm sorry, but you'll have to go," a nurse was saying. They were being whisked out. Meredith fought as she was forced out into the hall.

"Granddaddy—!"

"*Vampire!*" that unearthly voice wailed on.

And then: "White ash wood! Vampire! White ash wood—"

The door slammed shut.

Meredith gasped, fighting tears. Bonnie had her nails dug into Matt's arm. Stefan turned to them, green eyes wide with shock.

"I *said*, you'll have to leave now," the harassed nurse was repeating impatiently. The four of them ignored her. They were all looking at each other, stunned confusion giving way to realization in their faces.

"Tyler said there was only one kind of wood that could hurt him—" Matt began.

"*White ash wood*," said Stefan.

"We'll have to find out where he's hiding," Stefan said on the way home. He was driving, since Meredith had dropped the keys at the car door. "That's the first thing. If we rush this, we could warn him off."

His green eyes were shining with a queer mixture of triumph and grim determination, and he spoke in a clipped and rapid voice. They were all on the ragged edge, Bonnie thought, as if they'd been gulping uppers all night. Their nerves were frayed so thin that anything could happen.

She had a sense, too, of impending cataclysm. As if everything were coming to a head, all the events since Meredith's birthday party gathering to a conclusion.

Tonight, she thought. Tonight it all happens. It seemed strangely appropriate that it should be the eve of the solstice.

"The eve of what?" Matt said.

She hadn't even realized she'd spoken aloud. "The eve of the solstice," she said. "That's what today is. The day before the summer solstice."

"Don't tell me. Druids, right?"

"They celebrated it," Bonnie confirmed. "It's a day for magic, for marking the change of the seasons. And . . ." she hesitated. "Well, it's like all other feast days, like Halloween or the winter solstice. A day when the line between the visible world and the invisible world is thin. When you can see ghosts, they used to say. When things happen."

"Things," Stefan said, turning onto the main highway that headed back toward Fell's Church, "are going to happen."

None of them realized how soon.

Mrs. Flowers was in the back garden. They had driven straight to the boarding house to look for her. She was pruning rosebushes, and the smell of summer surrounded her.

She frowned and blinked when they all

crowded around her and asked her in a rush where to find a white ash tree.

"Slow down, slow down now," she said, peering at them from under the brim of her straw hat. "What is it you want? White ash? There's one just down beyond those oak trees in back. Now, wait a minute—" she added as they all scrambled off again.

Stefan ringed a branch of the tree with a jackknife Matt produced from his pocket. I wonder when he started carrying *that*? Bonnie thought. She also wondered what Mrs. Flowers thought of them as they came back, the two boys carrying the leafy six-foot bough between them on their shoulders.

But Mrs. Flowers just looked without saying anything. As they neared the house, though, she called after them, "A package came for you, boy."

Stefan turned his head, the branch still on his shoulder. "For *me*?"

"It had your name on it. A package and a letter. I found them on the front porch this afternoon. I put them upstairs in your room."

Bonnie looked at Meredith, then at Matt and Stefan, meeting their bewildered, suspicious gazes in turn. The anticipation in the air heightened suddenly, almost unbearably.

"But who could it be from? Who could even

know you're here—" she began as they climbed the stairs to the attic. And then she stopped, dread fluttering between her ribs. Premonition was buzzing around inside her like a nagging fly, but she pushed it away. Not now, she thought, not now.

But there was no way to keep from seeing the package on Stefan's desk. The boys propped the white ash branch against the wall and went to look at it, a longish, flattish parcel wrapped in brown paper, with a creamy envelope on top.

On the front, in familiar crazy handwriting, was scrawled *Stefan*.

The handwriting from the mirror.

They all stood staring down at the package as if it were a scorpion.

"Watch out," Meredith said as Stefan slowly reached for it. Bonnie knew what she meant. She felt as if the whole thing might explode or belch poisonous gas or turn into something with teeth and claws.

The envelope Stefan picked up was square and sturdy, made of good paper with a fine finish. Like a prince's invitation to the ball, Bonnie thought. But incongruously, there were several dirty fingerprints on the surface and the edges were grimy. Well—Klaus hadn't looked any too clean in the dream.

Stefan glanced at front and back and then

tore the envelope open. He pulled out a single piece of heavy stationery. The other three crowded around, looking over his shoulder as he unfolded it. Then Matt gave an exclamation.

"What the . . . it's blank!"

It was. On both sides. Stefan turned it over and examined each. His face was tense, shuttered. Everyone else relaxed, though, making noises of disgust. A stupid practical joke. Meredith had reached for the package, which looked flat enough to be empty as well, when Stefan suddenly stiffened, his breath hissing in. Bonnie glanced quickly over and jumped. Meredith's hand froze on the package, and Matt swore.

On the blank paper, held tautly between Stefan's two hands, letters were appearing. They were black with long downstrokes, as if each were being slashed by an invisible knife while Bonnie watched. As she read them, the dread inside her grew.

Stefan—

Shall we try to solve this like gentlemen? I have the girl. Come to the old farmhouse in the woods after dark and we'll talk, just the two of us. Come alone and I'll let her go. Bring anyone else and she dies.

There was no signature, but at the bottom the words appeared *This is between you and me.*

"What girl?" Matt was demanding, looking from Bonnie to Meredith as if to make sure they were still there. "What girl?"

With a sharp motion, Meredith's elegant fingers tore the package open and pulled out what was inside. A pale green scarf with a pattern of vines and leaves. Bonnie remembered it perfectly, and a vision came to her in a rush. Confetti and birthday presents, orchids and chocolate.

"Caroline," she whispered, and shut her eyes.

These last two weeks had been so strange, so different from ordinary high school life, that she had almost forgotten Caroline existed. Caroline had gone off to an apartment in another town to escape, to be safe—but Meredith had said it to her in the beginning. *He can follow you to Heron, I'm sure.*

"He was just playing with us again," Bonnie murmured. "He let us get this far, even going to see your grandfather, Meredith, and then . . ."

"He must have known," Meredith agreed. "He must have known all along we were looking for a victim. And now he's checkmated us. Unless—" Her dark eyes lit with sudden hope. "Bonnie, you don't think Caroline could have dropped this scarf the night of the party? And that he just picked it up?"

"No." The premonition was buzzing closer

and Bonnie swatted at it, trying to keep it away. She didn't *want* it, didn't want to know. But she felt certain of one thing: this wasn't a bluff. Klaus had Caroline.

"What are we going to do?" she said softly.

"I know what we're *not* going to do, and that's listen to *him*," Matt said. " 'Try to solve it like gentlemen'—he's scum, not a gentleman. It's a trap."

"Of course it's a trap," Meredith said impatiently. "He waited until we found out how to hurt him and now he's trying to separate us. But it won't work!"

Bonnie had been watching Stefan's face with growing dismay. Because while Matt and Meredith were indignantly talking, he had been quietly folding up the letter and putting it back in its envelope. Now he stood gazing down at it, his face still, untouched by anything that was going on around him. And the look in his green eyes scared Bonnie.

"We can make it backfire on him," Matt was saying. "Right, Stefan? Don't you think?"

"I think," said Stefan carefully, concentrating on each word, "that I am going out to the woods after dark."

Matt nodded, and like the quarterback he was, began to chart out a plan. "Okay, you go distract him. And meanwhile, the three of us—"

"The three of you," Stefan continued just as deliberately, looking right at him, "are going home. To bed."

There was a pause that seemed endless to Bonnie's taut nerves. The others just stared at Stefan.

At last Meredith said lightly, "Well, it's going to be hard to catch him while we're in bed unless he's kind enough to come visiting."

That broke the tension and Matt said, drawing a long-suffering breath, "All right, Stefan, I understand how you feel about this—" But Stefan interrupted.

"I'm dead serious, Matt. Klaus is right; this is between him and me. And he says to come alone or he'll hurt Caroline. So I'm going alone. It's my decision."

"It's your *funeral*," Bonnie blurted out, almost hysterically. "Stefan, you're crazy. You *can't*."

"Watch me."

"We won't *let* you—"

"Do you think," Stefan said, looking at her, "that you could stop me if you tried?"

This silence was acutely uncomfortable. Staring at him, Bonnie felt as if Stefan had changed somehow before her eyes. His face seemed sharper, his posture different, as if to remind her of the lithe, hard predator's muscles under his clothes. All at once he seemed distant, alien. Frightening.

Bonnie looked away.

"Let's be reasonable about this," Matt was saying, changing tactics. "Let's just stay calm and talk this over—"

"There's nothing to talk over. I'm going. You're not."

"You owe us more than that, Stefan," Meredith said, and Bonnie felt grateful for her cool voice. "Okay, so you can tear us all limb from limb; fine, no argument. We get the point. But after all we've been through together, we deserve more of a thorough discussion before you go running off."

"You said it was the girls' fight too," Matt added. "When did you decide it wasn't?"

"When I found out who the killer was!" Stefan said. "It's because of me that Klaus is here."

"No, it isn't!" Bonnie cried. "Did you make Elena kill Katherine?"

"I made Katherine go back to Klaus! *That's* how this got started. And I got Caroline involved; if it wasn't for me, she would never have hated Elena, never have gotten in with Tyler. I have a responsibility toward her."

"You just *want* to believe that," Bonnie almost yelled. "Klaus hates all of us! Do you really think he's going to let you walk out of there? Do you think he plans to leave the rest of us alone?"

"No," Stefan said, and picked up the branch leaning against the wall. He took Matt's knife out of his own pocket and began to strip the twigs off, making it into a straight white spear.

"Oh, great, you're going off for single combat!" Matt said, furious. "Don't you see how stupid that is? You're walking right into his trap!" He advanced a step on Stefan. "You may not think that the three of us can stop you—"

"No, Matt." Meredith's low, level voice cut across the room. "It won't do any good." Stefan looked at her, the muscles around his eyes hardening, but she just looked back, her face set and calm. "So you're determined to meet Klaus face to face, Stefan. All right. But before you go, at least be sure you have a fighting chance." Coolly, she began to unbutton the neck of her tailored blouse.

Bonnie felt a jolt, even though she'd offered the same thing only a week earlier. But that had been in private, for God's sake, she thought. Then she shrugged. Public or private, what difference did it make?

She looked at Matt, whose face reflected his consternation. Then she saw Matt's brow crease and the beginning of that stubborn, bullheaded expression that used to terrify the coaches of opposing football teams. His blue eyes turned to hers and she nodded, thrusting out her chin. Without a word, she unzipped the light windbreaker she was wearing and Matt pulled off his T-shirt.

Stefan stared from one to another of the three people grimly disrobing in his room, trying to conceal his own shock. But he shook his head, the white spear in front of him like a weapon. "No."

"Don't be a jerk, Stefan," Matt snapped. Even in the confusion of this terrible moment something inside Bonnie paused to admire his bare chest. "There's three of us. You should be able to take plenty without hurting any one of us."

"I said, no! Not for revenge, and not to fight evil with evil! Not for any reason. I thought *you* would understand that." Stefan's look at Matt was bitter.

"I understand that you're going to die out there!" Matt shouted.

"He's right!" Bonnie pressed her knuckles against her lips. The premonition was getting through her defenses. She didn't want to let it in, but she didn't have the strength to resist anymore. With a shudder, she felt it stab through and heard the words in her mind.

"*No one can fight him and live*," she said painfully. "That's what Vickie said, and it's true. I *feel* it, Stefan. No one can fight him and live!"

For a moment, just a moment, she thought he might listen to her. Then his face went hard again and he spoke coldly.

"It isn't your problem. Let me worry about it."

"But if there's no way to win—" Matt began.

"That isn't what Bonnie said!" Stefan replied tersely.

"Yes, it is! What the hell are you talking about?" Matt shouted. It was hard to make Matt lose his temper, but once lost it wasn't easily gotten back. "Stefan, I've had enough—"

"And so have I!" Stefan shot back in a roar. In a tone Bonnie had never heard him use before. "I'm sick of you all, sick of your bickering and your spinelessness—and your premonitions, too! This is *my* problem."

"I thought we were a team—" Matt cried.

"We are not a *team*. *You* are a bunch of stupid humans! Even with everything that's happened to you, deep down you just want to live your safe little lives in your safe little houses until you go to your safe little graves! I'm nothing like you and I don't want to be! I've put up with you this long because I had to, but this is the end." He looked at each of them and spoke deliberately, emphasizing each word. "I don't need any of you. I don't want you with me, and I don't want you following me. You'll only spoil my strategy. Anyone who *does* follow me, I'll kill."

And with one last smoldering glance, he turned on his heel and walked out.

Fourteen

"He's gone round the bend," Matt said, staring at the empty doorway through which Stefan had disappeared.

"No, he hasn't," said Meredith. Her voice was rueful and quiet, but there was a kind of helpless laugh in it too. "Don't you see what he's doing, Matt?" she said when he turned to her. "Yelling at us, making us hate him to try and chase us away. Being as nasty as possible so we'll stay mad and let him do this alone." She glanced at the doorway and raised her eyebrows. " 'Anyone who does follow me, I'll kill' *was* going a bit overboard, though."

Bonnie giggled suddenly, wildly, in spite of herself. "I think he borrowed it from Damon. 'Get this straight, I don't need any of you!' "

" 'You bunch of stupid humans,' " Matt added.

"But I still don't understand. You just had a premonition, Bonnie, and Stefan doesn't usually discount those. If there's no way to fight and win, what's the point of going?"

"Bonnie didn't say there was no way to fight and win. She said there was no way to fight and *survive*. Right, Bonnie?" Meredith looked at her.

The fit of giggles dissolved away. Startled herself, Bonnie tried to examine the premonition, but she knew no more than the words that had sprung into her mind. *No one can fight him and live*.

"You mean Stefan thinks—" Slow, thunderous outrage was smoldering in Matt's eyes. "He thinks he's going to go and stop Klaus even though he gets killed himself? Like some sacrificial lamb?"

"More like Elena," Meredith said soberly. "And maybe—so he can be with her."

"Huh-uh." Bonnie shook her head. She might not know more about the prophecy, but *this* she knew. "He doesn't think that, I'm sure. Elena's special. She is what she is because she died too young; she left so much unfinished in her own life, and—well, she's a special case. But Stefan's been a vampire for five hundred years, and he certainly wouldn't be dying young. There's no guarantee he'd end up with Elena. He might go to another place or—or just *go out*. And he knows that. I'm sure he knows that. I think he's just keeping his promise to her, to stop Klaus no matter what it costs."

"To try, at least," Matt said softly, and it sounded as if he were quoting. "Even if you know you're going to lose." He looked up at the girls suddenly. "I'm going after him."

"Of course," said Meredith patiently.

Matt hesitated. "Uh—I don't suppose I could convince you two to stay here?"

"After all that inspiring talk about teamwork? Not a chance."

"I was afraid of that. So . . ."

"So," said Bonnie, "we're out of here."

They gathered what weapons they could. Matt's pocketknife that Stefan had dropped, the ivory-hilted dagger from Stefan's dresser, a carving knife from the kitchen.

Outside, there was no sign of Mrs. Flowers. The sky was pale purple, shading to apricot in the west. Twilight of the solstice eve, Bonnie thought, and hairs on her arms tried to lift.

"Klaus said the old farmhouse in the woods—that must mean the Francher place," Matt said. "Where Katherine dumped Stefan in the abandoned well."

"That makes sense. He's probably been using Katherine's tunnel to get back and forth under the river," Meredith said. "Unless Old Ones are so powerful they can cross running water without harming themselves."

That's right, Bonnie remembered, evil things couldn't cross running water, and the more evil you were, the harder it was. "But we don't know anything about the Originals," she said aloud.

"No, and that means we've got to be careful," Matt said. "I know these woods pretty well, and I know the path Stefan will probably use. I think we should take a different one."

"So Stefan won't see us and kill us?"

"So *Klaus* won't see us, or not all of us. So maybe we'll have a chance of getting to Caroline. Somehow or other we've got to get Caroline out of the equation; as long as Klaus can threaten to hurt her he can make Stefan do anything he wants. And it's always best to plan ahead, to get a jump on the enemy. Klaus said meet there after dark; well, we'll be there *before* dark and maybe we can surprise him."

Bonnie was deeply impressed by this strategy. No wonder he's a quarterback, she was thinking. I would have just rushed in, yelling.

Matt picked out an almost invisible path between the oak trees. The undergrowth was especially lush this time of year, with mosses, grasses, flowering plants, and ferns. Bonnie had to trust that Matt knew where he was going, because *she* certainly didn't. Above, birds were giving one last burst of song before seeking out a roost for the night.

It got dimmer. Moths and lacewings fluttered past Bonnie's face. After stumbling through a patch of toadstools covered with feeding slugs, she was intensely grateful that this time she'd worn jeans.

At last Matt stopped them. "We're getting close," he said, his voice low. "There's a sort of bluff where we can look down and Klaus might not see us. Be quiet and careful."

Bonnie had never taken so much trouble placing her feet before. Fortunately the leaf litter was wet and not crackly. After a few minutes Matt dropped to his stomach and gestured for them to follow. Bonnie kept telling herself, fiercely, that she didn't mind the centipedes and earthworms her sliding fingers dug up, that she had no feelings one way or another about cobwebs in the face. This was life and death, and she was *competent*. No dweeb, no baby, but *competent*.

"Here," Matt whispered, his voice barely audible. Bonnie scooted on her stomach up to him and looked.

They were gazing down on the Francher homestead—or what was left of it. It had crumbled into the earth long ago, taken back by the forest. Now it was only a foundation, building stones covered with flowering weeds and prickly brambles, and one tall chimney like a lonely monument.

"There she is. Caroline," Meredith breathed in Bonnie's other ear.

Caroline was a dim figure sitting against the chimney. Her pale green dress showed up in the gathering dark, but her auburn hair just looked black. Something white shone across her face, and after a moment Bonnie realized it was a gag. Tape or a bandage. From her strange posture—arms behind her, legs stretched straight out in front—Bonnie also guessed she was tied.

Poor Caroline, she thought, forgiving the other girl all the nasty, petty, selfish things she'd ever done, which was a pretty considerable amount when you got down to it. But Bonnie couldn't imagine anything worse than being abducted by a psycho vampire who'd already killed two of your classmates, dragged out here to the woods and bound, and then left to wait, with your life depending on another vampire who had fairly good reason to hate you. After all, Caroline had wanted Stefan in the beginning, and had hated and tried to humiliate Elena for getting him. Stefan Salvatore was the last person who should feel kindly toward Caroline Forbes.

"Look!" said Matt. "Is that him? Klaus?"

Bonnie had seen it too, a ripple of movement

on the opposite side of the chimney. As she strained her eyes he appeared, his light tan raincoat flapping ghostlike around his legs. He glanced down at Caroline and she shrank from him, trying to lean away. His laughter sounded so clearly in the quiet air that Bonnie flinched.

"That's him," she whispered, dropping down behind the screening ferns. "But where's Stefan? It's almost dark now."

"Maybe he got smart and decided not to come," said Matt.

"No such luck," said Meredith. She was looking through the ferns to the south. Bonnie glanced that way herself and started.

Stefan was standing at the edge of the clearing, having materialized there as if out of thin air. Not even Klaus had seen him coming, Bonnie thought. He stood silently, making no attempt to hide himself or the white ash spear he was carrying. There was something in his stance and the way he looked over the scene before him that made Bonnie remember that in the fifteenth century he'd been an aristocrat, a member of the nobility. He said nothing, waiting for Klaus to notice him, refusing to be rushed.

When Klaus did turn south he went still, and Bonnie got the feeling he was surprised Stefan had sneaked up on him. But then he laughed and spread his arms.

"Salvatore! What a coincidence; I was just thinking about you!"

Slowly, Stefan looked Klaus up and down, from the tails of his tattered raincoat to the top of his windblown head. What Stefan said was:

"You asked for me. I'm here. Let the girl go."

"Did I say that?" Looking genuinely surprised, Klaus pressed two hands to his chest. Then he shook his head, chuckling. "I don't think so. Let's talk first."

Stefan nodded, as if Klaus had confirmed something bitter he'd been expecting. He took the spear from his shoulder and held it in front of him, handling the unwieldy length of wood deftly, easily. "I'm listening," he said.

"Not as dumb as he looks," Matt murmured from behind the ferns, a note of respect in his voice. "And he's not as anxious to get killed as I thought," Matt added. "He's being careful."

Klaus gestured toward Caroline, the tips of his fingers brushing her auburn hair. "Why don't you come here so we don't have to shout?" But he didn't threaten to hurt his prisoner, Bonnie noticed.

"I can hear you just fine," Stefan replied.

"Good," Matt whispered. "That's it, Stefan!"

Bonnie, though, was studying Caroline. The captive girl was struggling, tossing her head back and forth as if she were frantic or in pain. But

Bonnie got a strange feeling about Caroline's movements, especially those violent jerks of the head, as if the girl was straining to reach the sky. The sky . . . Bonnie's gaze lifted up to it, where full darkness had fallen and a waning moon shone over the trees. That was why she could see that Caroline's hair was auburn now: the moonlight, she thought. Then, with a shock, her eyes dropped to the tree just above Stefan, whose branches were rustling slightly in the absence of any wind. "Matt?" she whispered, alarmed.

Stefan was focused on Klaus, every sense, every muscle, every atom of his Power honed and turned toward the Old One before him. But in that tree directly above him . . .

All thoughts of strategy, of asking Matt what to do, fled from Bonnie's mind. She bolted up from her place of concealment and shouted.

"Stefan! Above you! It's a trap!"

Stefan leaped aside, neat as a cat, just as something plunged down on the exact place he'd been standing an instant before. The moon lit the scene perfectly, enough for Bonnie to see the white of Tyler's bared teeth.

And to see the white flash of Klaus's eyes as he whirled on her. For one stunned instant she stared at him, and then lightning crackled.

From an empty sky.

It was only later that Bonnie would realize the strangeness—the fearsomeness—of this. At the time she scarcely noted that the sky was clear and star swept and that the jagged blue bolt that forked down struck the palm of Klaus's upraised hand. The next sight she saw was so terrifying as to black everything else out: Klaus folding his hand over that lightning, *gathering* it somehow, and throwing it at her.

Stefan was yelling, telling her to get away, *get away!* Bonnie heard him while she stared, paralyzed, and then something grabbed her and wrenched her aside. The bolt snapped over her head, with a sound like a giant whip cracking and a smell like ozone. She landed facedown in moss and rolled over to grasp Meredith's hand and thank Meredith for saving her, only to find that it was Matt.

"Stay here! Right here!" he shouted, and bounded away.

Those dreaded words. They catapulted Bonnie right up, and she was running after him before she knew what she was doing.

And then the world turned into chaos.

Klaus had whirled back on Stefan, who was grappling with Tyler, beating him. Tyler, in his wolf form, was making terrible sounds as Stefan threw him to the ground.

Meredith was running toward Caroline, approaching from behind the chimney so Klaus wouldn't spot her. Bonnie saw her reach Caroline and saw the flash of Stefan's silver dagger as Meredith cut the cords around Caroline's wrists. Then Meredith was half carrying, half dragging Caroline behind the chimney to work on her feet.

A sound like antlers clashing made Bonnie spin around. Klaus had come at Stefan with a tall branch of his own—it must have been lying flat on the ground before. It looked just as sharp as Stefan's, making it a serviceable lance. But Klaus and Stefan weren't just stabbing at each other; they were using the sticks as quarterstaffs. Robin Hood, Bonnie thought dazedly. Little John and Robin. That was what it looked like: Klaus was that much taller and heavier boned than Stefan.

Then Bonnie saw something else and cried out wordlessly. Behind Stefan, Tyler had gotten up again and was crouching, just as he had in the graveyard before lunging for Stefan's throat. Stefan's back was to him. And Bonnie couldn't warn him in time.

But she'd forgotten about Matt. Head down, ignoring claws and fangs, he was charging at Tyler, tackling him like a first-rate linebacker before he could leap. Tyler went flying sideways, with Matt on top of him.

Bonnie was overwhelmed. So much was happening. Meredith was sawing through Caroline's ankle cords; Matt was pummeling Tyler in a way that certainly would have gotten him disqualified on the football field; Stefan was whirling that white ash staff as if he'd been trained for it. Klaus was laughing deliriously, seeming exhilarated by the exercise, as they traded blows with deadly speed and accuracy.

But Matt seemed to be in trouble now. Tyler was gripping him and snarling, trying to get a hold on his throat. Wildly, Bonnie looked around for a weapon, entirely forgetting the carving knife in her pocket. Her eye fell on a dead oak branch. She picked it up and ran to where Tyler and Matt were struggling.

Once there, though, she faltered. She didn't dare use the stick for fear she'd hit Matt with it. He and Tyler were rolling over and over in a blur of motion.

Then Matt was on top of Tyler again, holding Tyler's head down, holding himself clear. Bonnie saw her chance and aimed the stick. But Tyler saw *her*. With a burst of supernatural strength, he gathered his legs and sent Matt soaring off him backward. Matt's head struck a tree with a sound Bonnie would never forget. The dull sound of a rotten melon bursting. He slid down the front of the tree and was still.

Bonnie was gasping, stunned. She might have started toward Matt, but Tyler was there in front of her, breathing hard, bloody saliva running down his chin. He looked even more like an animal than he had in the graveyard. As if in a dream, Bonnie raised her stick, but she could feel it shaking in her hands. Matt was so still—was he breathing? Bonnie could hear the sob in her own breath as she faced Tyler. This was ridiculous; this was a boy from her own school. A boy she'd danced with last year at the Junior Prom. How could he be keeping her away from Matt, how could he be trying to hurt them all? How could he be *doing* this?

"Tyler, please—" she began, meaning to reason with him, to beg him . . .

"All alone in the woods, little girl?" he said, and his voice was a thick and guttural growl, shaped at the last minute into words. In that instant Bonnie knew that this was not the boy she'd gone to school with. This was an *animal*. Oh, God, he's ugly, she thought. Ropes of red spit hung out of his mouth. And those yellow eyes with the slitted pupils—in them she saw the cruelty of the shark, and the crocodile, and the wasp that lays its eggs in a caterpillar's living body. All the cruelty of animal nature in those two yellow eyes.

"Somebody should have warned you," Tyler

said, dropping his jaw to laugh the way a dog does. "Because if you go out in the woods alone, you might meet the Big Bad—"

"Jerk!" a voice finished for him, and with a feeling of gratitude that bordered on the religious, Bonnie saw Meredith beside her. Meredith, holding Stefan's dagger, which shone liquidly in the moonlight.

"Silver, Tyler," Meredith said, brandishing it. "I wonder what silver does to a werewolf's members? Want to see?" All Meredith's elegance, her standoffishness, her cool observer's dispassion were gone. This was the essential Meredith, a warrior Meredith, and although she was smiling, she was *mad*.

"*Yes!*" shouted Bonnie gleefully, feeling power rush through her. Suddenly she could move. She and Meredith, together, were strong. Meredith was stalking Tyler from one side, Bonnie held her stick ready on the other. A longing she'd never felt before shot through her, the longing to hit Tyler so hard his head would come flying off. She could feel the strength to do it surging in her arm.

And Tyler, with his animal instinct, could sense it, could sense it from both of them, closing in on either side. He recoiled, caught himself, and turned to try and get away from them. They turned too. In a minute they were all three orbiting like a mini solar system: Tyler turning around and around in the middle; Bonnie and Meredith circling him, looking for a chance to attack.

One, two, *three*. Some unspoken signal flashed from Meredith to Bonnie. Just as Tyler leaped at Meredith, trying to knock the knife aside, Bonnie hit. Remembering the advice of a distant boyfriend who'd tried to teach her to play baseball, she imagined not just hitting Tyler's head but *through* his head, hitting something on the opposite side. She put the whole weight of her small body behind the blow, and the shock of connecting nearly jarred her teeth loose. It jolted her arms agonizingly and it shattered the stick. But Tyler fell like a bird shot out of the sky.

"I did it! *Yes! All right! Yes!*" Bonnie shouted, flinging the stick away. Triumph erupted from her in a primal shout. "*We did it!*" She grabbed the heavy body by the back of the mane and pulled it off Meredith, where it had fallen. "*We—*"

Then she broke off, her words freezing in her throat. "*Meredith!*" she cried.

"It's all right," Meredith gasped, her voice tight with pain. And weakness, Bonnie thought, chilled as if doused with ice water. Tyler had clawed her leg to the bone. There were huge, gaping wounds in the thigh of Meredith's jeans and in the white skin that showed clearly through the torn cloth. And to Bonnie's absolute horror, she could see inside the skin too, could see flesh and muscle ripped and red blood pouring out.

"Meredith—" she cried frantically. They had to get Meredith to a doctor. Everyone had to stop now; everyone must understand that. They had an injury here; they needed to get an ambulance, to call 911. "Meredith," she gasped, almost weeping.

"Tie it up with something." Meredith's face was white. Shock. Going into shock. And so much blood; so much blood coming out. Oh, God, thought Bonnie, please help me. She looked for something to tie it up with, but there was nothing.

Something dropped on the ground beside her. A length of nylon cord like the cord they'd used to tie up Tyler, with frayed edges. Bonnie looked up.

"Can you use that?" asked Caroline uncertainly, her teeth chattering.

She was wearing the green dress, her auburn hair straggling and stuck to her face with sweat and blood. Even as she spoke she swayed, and fell to her knees beside Meredith.

"Are *you* hurt?" Bonnie gasped.

Caroline shook her head, but then she bent forward, racked with nausea, and Bonnie saw the marks in her throat. But there was no time to worry about Caroline now. Meredith was more important.

Bonnie tied the cord above Meredith's wounds, her mind running desperately over things she'd learned from her sister Mary. Mary was a nurse. Mary said—a tourniquet couldn't be too tight or left on too long or gangrene set in. But she had to stop the gushing blood. Oh, Meredith.

"Bonnie—help Stefan," Meredith was gasping, her voice almost a whisper. "He's going to need it. . . ." She sagged backward, her breathing stertorous, her slitted eyes looking up at the sky.

Wet. Everything was wet. Bonnie's hands, her clothes, the ground. Wet with Meredith's blood. And Matt was still lying under the tree, unconscious. She couldn't leave them, especially not with Tyler there. He might wake up.

Dazed, she turned to Caroline, who was shivering and retching, sweat beading her face. Useless, Bonnie thought. But she had no other choice.

"Caroline, listen to me," she said. She picked up the largest piece of the stick she'd used on Tyler and put it into Caroline's hands. "You stay with Matt and Meredith. Loosen that tourniquet every twenty minutes or so. And if Tyler starts to wake up, if he even *twitches*, you hit him as hard as you can with this. Understand? Caroline," she added, "this is your big chance to prove you're good for something. That you're not useless. All right?" She caught the furtive green eyes and repeated, "All right?"

"But what are *you* going to do?"

Bonnie looked toward the clearing.

"No, Bonnie." Caroline's hand grasped her, and Bonnie noted with some part of her mind the broken nails, the rope burns on the wrists. "Stay here where it's safe. Don't go to them. There's nothing you can do—"

Bonnie shook her off and made for the clearing before she lost her resolve. In her heart, she knew Caroline was right. There was nothing she could do. But something Matt had said before they left was ringing in her mind. To try at least. She had to try.

Still, in those next few horrible minutes all she could do was look.

So far, Stefan and Klaus had been trading blows with such violence and accuracy that it had been like a beautiful, lethal dance. But it had been an equal, or almost equal, match. Stefan had been holding his own.

Now she saw Stefan bearing down with his

white ash lance, pressing Klaus to his knees, forcing him backward, farther and farther back, like a limbo dancer seeing how low he could go. And Bonnie could see Klaus's face now, mouth slightly open, staring up at Stefan with what looked like astonishment and fear.

Then everything changed.

At the very bottom of his descent, when Klaus had bent back as far as he could go, when it seemed that he must be about to collapse or break, something happened.

Klaus smiled.

And then he started pushing back.

Bonnie saw Stefan's muscles knot, saw his arms go rigid, trying to resist. But Klaus, still grinning madly, eyes wide open, just kept coming. He unfolded like some terrible jack-in-the-box, only slowly. Slowly. Inexorably. His grin getting wider until it looked as if it would split his face. Like the Cheshire cat.

A cat, thought Bonnie.

Cat with a mouse.

Now Stefan was the one grunting and straining, teeth clenched, trying to hold Klaus off. But Klaus and his stick bore down, forcing Stefan backward, forcing him to the ground.

Grinning all the time.

Until Stefan was lying on his back, his own stick pressing into his throat with the weight of

Klaus's lance across it. Klaus looked down at him and beamed. "I'm tired of playing, little boy," he said, and he straightened and threw his own stick down. "Now it's dying time."

He took Stefan's staff away from him as easily as if he were taking it from a child. Picked it up with a flick of his wrist and broke it over his knee, showing how strong he was, how strong he had always been. How cruelly he had been playing with Stefan.

One of the halves of the white ash stick he tossed over his shoulder across the clearing. The other he jabbed at Stefan. Using not the pointed end but the splintered one, broken into a dozen tiny points. He jabbed down with a force that seemed almost casual, but Stefan screamed. He did it again and again, eliciting a scream each time.

Bonnie cried out, soundlessly.

She had never heard Stefan scream before. She didn't need to be told what kind of pain must have caused it. She didn't need to be told that white ash might be the only wood deadly to Klaus, but that any wood was deadly to Stefan. That Stefan was, if not dying now, about to die. That Klaus, with his hand now raised, was going to finish it with one more plunging blow. Klaus's face was tilted to the moon in a grin of obscene pleasure, showing that *this* was what he liked, where he got his thrills. From killing.

And Bonnie couldn't move, couldn't even cry. The world swam around her. It had all been a mistake, she wasn't competent; she was a baby after all. She didn't want to see that final thrust, but she couldn't look away. And all this couldn't be happening, but it was. It was.

Klaus flourished the splintered stake and with a smile of pure ecstasy started to bring it down.

And a spear shot across the clearing and struck him in the middle of the back, landing and quivering like a giant arrow, like half a giant arrow. It made Klaus's arms fling out, dropping the stake; it shocked the ecstatic grin right off his face. He stood, arms extended, for a second, and then turned, the white ash stick in his back wobbling slightly.

Bonnie's eyes were too dazzled by waves of gray dots to see, but she heard the voice clearly as it rang out, cold and arrogant and filled with absolute conviction. Just five words, but they changed everything.

"*Get away from my brother.*"

Fifteen

Klaus screamed, a scream that reminded Bonnie of ancient predators, of the sabertooth cat and the bull mammoth. Blood frothed out of his mouth along with the scream, turning that handsome face into a twisted mask of fury.

His hands scrabbled at his back, trying to get a grip on the white ash stake and pull it out. But it was buried too deep. The throw had been a good one.

"Damon," Bonnie whispered.

He was standing at the edge of the clearing, framed by oak trees. As she watched, he took a step toward Klaus, and then another; lithe stalking steps filled with deadly purpose.

And he was angry. Bonnie would have run from the look on his face if her muscles hadn't been frozen. She had never seen such menace so barely held in check.

"Get . . . away . . . from my brother," he said, almost breathing it, with his eyes never leaving Klaus's as he took another step.

Klaus screamed again, but his hands stopped their frantic scrabbling. "You idiot! We don't have to fight! I told you that at the house! We can ignore each other!"

Damon's voice was no louder than before. "Get away from my brother." Bonnie could feel it inside him, a swell of Power like a tsunami. He continued, so softly that Bonnie had to strain to hear him, "Before I tear your heart out."

Bonnie could move after all. She stepped backward.

"I told you!" screamed Klaus, frothing. Damon didn't acknowledge the words in any way. His whole being seemed focused on Klaus's throat, on his chest, on the beating heart inside that he was going to tear out.

Klaus picked up the unbroken lance and rushed him.

In spite of all the blood, the blond man seemed to have plenty of strength left. The rush was sudden, violent, and almost inescapable. Bonnie saw him thrust the lance at Damon and shut her eyes involuntarily, and then opened them an instant later as she heard the flurry of wings.

Klaus had plunged right through the spot where Damon had been, and a black crow was soaring upward while a single feather floated down. As Bonnie stared, Klaus's rush took him into the darkness beyond the clearing and he disappeared.

Dead silence fell in the wood.

Bonnie's paralysis broke slowly, and she first stepped, and then ran to where Stefan lay. He didn't open his eyes at her approach; he seemed unconscious. She knelt beside him. And then she felt a sort of horrible calm creep over her, like someone who has been swimming in ice water and at last feels the first undeniable signs of hypothermia. If she hadn't had so many successive shocks already, she might have fled screaming or dissolved into hysterics. But as it was, this was simply the last step, the last little slide into unreality. Into a world that couldn't be, but was.

Because it was bad. Very bad. As bad as it could be.

She'd never seen anybody hurt like this. Not even Mr. Tanner, and he had died of his wounds. Nothing Mary had ever said could help fix this. Even if they'd had Stefan on a stretcher outside an operating room, it wouldn't have been enough.

In that state of dreadful calm she looked up to see a flutter of wings blur and shimmer in the moonlight. Damon stood beside her, and she spoke quite collectedly and rationally.

"Will giving him blood help?"

He didn't seem to hear her. His eyes were all black, all pupil. That barely leashed violence, that sense of ferocious energy held back, was gone. He knelt and touched the dark head on the ground.

"Stefan?"

Bonnie shut her eyes.

Damon's scared, she thought. Damon's scared—*Damon!*—and oh, God, I don't know what to do. There's *nothing* to do—and it's all over and we're all lost and *Damon* is scared for Stefan. He isn't going to take care of things and he hasn't got a solution and somebody's got to fix this. And oh, God, please help me because I'm so frightened and Stefan's dying and Meredith and Matt are hurt and Klaus is going to come back.

She opened her eyes to look at Damon. He was white, his face looking terrifyingly young at that moment, with those dilated black eyes.

"Klaus is coming back," Bonnie said quietly. She wasn't afraid of him anymore. They weren't a centuries-old hunter and a seventeen-year-old human girl, sitting here at the edge of the world.

They were just two people, Damon and Bonnie, who had to do the best they could.

"I know," Damon said. He was holding Stefan's hand, looking completely unembarrassed about it, and it seemed quite logical and sensible. Bonnie could feel him sending Power into Stefan, could also feel that it wasn't enough.

"Would blood help him?"

"Not much. A little, maybe."

"Anything that helps at all we've got to try."

Stefan whispered, "No."

Bonnie was surprised. She'd thought he was unconscious. But his eyes were open now, open and alert and smoldering green. They were the only alive thing about him.

"Don't be stupid," Damon said, his voice hardening. He was gripping Stefan's hand until his knuckles whitened. "You're badly hurt."

"I won't break my promise." That immovable stubbornness was in Stefan's voice, in his pale face. And when Damon opened his mouth again, undoubtedly to say that Stefan would break it and like it or Damon would break his neck, Stefan added, "Especially when it won't do any good."

There was a silence while Bonnie fought with the raw truth of this. Where they were now, in this terrible place beyond all ordinary things, pretense or false reassurance seemed wrong.

Only the truth would do. And Stefan was telling the truth.

He was still looking at his brother, who was looking back, all that fierce, furious attention focused on Stefan as it had been focused on Klaus earlier. As if somehow that would help.

"I'm not badly hurt, I'm dead," Stefan said brutally, his eyes locked on Damon's. Their last and greatest struggle of wills, Bonnie thought. "And you need to get Bonnie and the others out of here."

"We won't leave you," Bonnie intervened. That was the truth; she could say that.

"You *have* to!" Stefan didn't glance aside, didn't look away from his brother. "Damon, you know I'm right. Klaus will be here any minute. Don't throw your life away. Don't throw *their* lives away."

"I don't give a damn about their lives," Damon hissed. The truth also, Bonnie thought, curiously unoffended. There was only one life Damon cared about here, and it wasn't his own.

"Yes, you do!" Stefan flared back. He was hanging on to Damon's hand with just as fierce a grip, as if this was a contest and he could force Damon to concede that way. "Elena had a last request; well, this is mine. You have Power, Damon. I want you to use it to help them."

"Stefan . . ." Bonnie whispered helplessly.

"*Promise me,*" Stefan said to Damon, and then a spasm of pain twisted his face.

For uncountable seconds Damon simply looked down at him. Then he said, "I promise," quick and sharp as the stroke of a dagger. He let go of Stefan's hand and stood, turning to Bonnie. "Come on."

"We can't *leave* him . . ."

"Yes, we can." There was nothing young about Damon's face now. Nothing vulnerable. "You and your human friends are leaving here, permanently. *I* am coming back."

Bonnie shook her head. She knew, dimly, that Damon wasn't betraying Stefan, that it was some case of Damon putting Stefan's ideals above Stefan's life, but it was all too abstruse and incomprehensible to her. She didn't understand it and she didn't want to. All she knew was that Stefan couldn't be left lying there.

"You're coming *now,*" Damon said, reaching for her, the steely ring back in his voice. Bonnie prepared herself for a fight, and then something happened that made all their debating meaningless. There was a crack like a giant whip and a flash like daylight, and Bonnie was blinded. When she could see through the afterimage, her eyes flew to the flames that were licking up from a newly blackened hole at the base of a tree.

Klaus had returned. With lightning.

Bonnie's eye darted to him next, as the only other thing moving in the clearing. He was waving the bloody white ash stake he'd pulled out of his own back like a gory trophy.

Lightning rod, thought Bonnie illogically, and then there was another crash.

It stabbed down from an empty sky, in huge blue-white forks that lit everything like the sun at noon. Bonnie watched as one tree and then another was hit, each one closer than the last. Flames licked up like hungry red goblins among the leaves.

Two trees on either side of Bonnie exploded, with cracks so loud that she felt rather than heard it, a piercing pain in her eardrums. Damon, whose eyes were more sensitive, threw up a hand to protect them.

Then he shouted "Klaus!" and sprang toward the blond man. He wasn't stalking now; this was the deadly race of attack. The burst of killing speed of the hunting cat or the wolf.

Lightning caught him in midspring.

Bonnie screamed as she saw it, jumping to her feet. There was a blue flash of superheated gases and a smell of burning, and then Damon was down, lying motionless on his face. Bonnie could see tiny wisps of smoke rise from him, just as they did from the trees.

Speechless with horror, she looked at Klaus.

He was swaggering through the clearing, holding his bloody stick like a golf club. He bent down over Damon as he passed, and smiled. Bonnie wanted to scream again, but she didn't have the breath. There didn't seem to be any air left to breathe.

"I'll deal with *you* later," Klaus told the unconscious Damon. Then his face tipped up toward Bonnie.

"You," he said, "I'm going to deal with right now."

It was an instant before she realized he was looking at Stefan, and not her. Those electric blue eyes were fixed on Stefan's face. They moved to Stefan's bloody middle.

"I'm going to *eat* you now, Salvatore."

Bonnie was all alone. The only one left standing. And she was afraid.

But she knew what she had to do.

She let her knees collapse again, dropping to the ground beside Stefan.

And this is how it ends, she thought. You kneel beside your knight and then you face the enemy.

She looked at Klaus and moved so that she was shielding Stefan. He seemed to notice her for the first time, and frowned as if he'd found a spider in his salad. Firelight flickered orange-red on his face.

"Get out of the way."

"No."

And this is how the ending starts. Like this, so simply, with one word, and you're going to die on a summer night. A summer night when the moon and stars are shining and bonfires burn like the flames the Druids used to summon the dead.

"Bonnie, go," Stefan said painfully. "Get out while you can."

"No," Bonnie said. I'm sorry, Elena, she thought. I can't save him. This is all I can do.

"Get out of the way," Klaus said through his teeth.

"No." She could wait and let Stefan die this way, instead of with Klaus's teeth in his throat. It might not seem like much of a difference, but it was the most she could offer.

"Bonnie . . ." Stefan whispered.

"Don't you know who I am, girl? I've walked with the devil. If you move, I'll let you die quickly."

Bonnie's voice had given out. She shook her head.

Klaus threw back his own head and laughed. A little more blood trickled out, too. "All right," he said. "Have it your own way. Both of you go together."

Summer night, Bonnie thought. The solstice eve. When the line between worlds is so thin.

"Say good night, sweetheart."

No time to trance, no time for anything. Nothing except one desperate appeal.

"*Elena!*" Bonnie screamed. "*Elena! Elena!*"

Klaus recoiled.

For an instant, it seemed as if the name alone had the power to alarm him. Or as if he expected something to respond to Bonnie's cry. He stood, listening.

Bonnie drew on her powers, putting everything she had into it, throwing her need and her call out into the void.

And felt . . . nothing.

Nothing disturbed the summer night except the crackling sound of flames. Klaus turned back to Bonnie and Stefan, and grinned.

Then Bonnie saw the mist creeping along the ground.

No—it couldn't be mist. It must be smoke from the fire. But it didn't behave like either. It was swirling, rising in the air like a tiny whirlwind or dust devil. It was gathering into a shape roughly the size of a man.

There was another one a little distance away. Then Bonnie saw a third. The same thing was happening all over.

Mist was flowing out of the ground, between

the trees. Pools of it, each separate and distinct. Bonnie, staring mutely, could see through each patch, could see the flames, the oak trees, the bricks of the chimney. Klaus had stopped smiling, stopped moving, and was watching too.

Bonnie turned to Stefan, unable to even frame the question.

"Unquiet spirits," he whispered huskily, his green eyes intent. "The solstice."

And then Bonnie understood.

They were coming. From across the river, where the old cemetery lay. From the woods, where countless makeshift graves had been dug to dump bodies in before they rotted. The unquiet spirits, the soldiers who had fought here and died during the Civil War. A supernatural host answering the call for help.

They were forming all around. There were hundreds of them.

Bonnie could actually see faces now. The misty outlines were filling in with pale hues like so many runny watercolors. She saw a flash of blue, a glimmer of gray. Both Union and Confederate troops. Bonnie glimpsed a pistol thrust into a belt, the glint of an ornamented sword. Chevrons on a sleeve. A bushy dark beard; a long, well-tended white one. A small figure, child size, with dark holes for eyes and a drum hanging at thigh level.

"Oh, my God," she whispered. "Oh, *God*." It wasn't swearing. It was something like a prayer.

Not that she wasn't frightened of them, because she was. It was every nightmare she'd ever had about the cemetery come true. Like her first dream about Elena, when things came crawling out of the black pits in the earth; only these things weren't crawling, they were *flying*, skimming and floating until they swirled into human form. Everything that Bonnie had ever felt about the old graveyard—that it was alive and full of watching eyes, that there was some Power lurking behind its waiting stillness—was proving true. The earth of Fell's Church was giving up its bloody memories. The spirits of those who'd died here were walking again.

And Bonnie could feel their anger. It frightened her, but another emotion was waking up inside her, making her catch her breath and clench tighter on Stefan's hand. Because the misty army had a leader.

One figure was floating in front of the others, closest to the place where Klaus stood. It had no shape or definition as yet, but it glowed and scintillated with the pale golden light of a candle flame. Then, before Bonnie's eyes, it seemed to take on substance from the air, shining brighter and brighter every minute with an unearthly light. It was brighter than the circle of fire. It was so bright that Klaus leaned back from it and Bonnie blinked, but when she turned at a low sound, she saw Stefan staring straight into it, fearlessly, with wide-open eyes. And smiling, so faintly, as if glad to have this be the last thing he saw.

Then Bonnie was sure.

Klaus dropped the stake. He had turned away from Bonnie and Stefan to face the being of light that hung in the clearing like an avenging angel. Golden hair streaming back in an invisible wind, Elena looked down on him.

"She came," Bonnie whispered.

"You asked her to," Stefan murmured. His voice trailed off into a labored breath, but he was still smiling. His eyes were serene.

"Stand away from them," Elena said, her voice coming simultaneously to Bonnie's ears and her mind. It was like the chiming of dozens of bells, distant and close up at once. "It's over now, Klaus."

But Klaus rallied quickly. Bonnie saw his shoulders swell with a breath, noticed for the first time the hole in the back of the tan raincoat where the white ash stake had pierced him. It was stained dull red, and new blood was flowing now as Klaus flung out his arms.

"You think I'm afraid of you?" he shouted. He spun around, laughing at all the pallid forms.

"You think I'm afraid of any of you? You're dead! Dust on the wind! You can't touch me!"

"You're wrong," Elena said in her wind-chime voice.

"I'm one of the Old Ones! An Original! Do you know what that means?" Klaus turned again, addressing all of them, his unnaturally blue eyes seeming to catch some of the red glow of the fire. "*I've never died.* Every one of you has died, you gallery of spooks! But not me. Death can't touch me. I am *invincible*!"

The last word came in a shout so loud it echoed among the trees. *Invincible . . . invincible . . . invincible.* Bonnie heard it fading into the hungry sound of the fire.

Elena waited until the last echo had died. Then she said, very simply, "Not quite." She turned to look at the misty shapes around her. "He wants to spill more blood here."

A new voice spoke up, a hollow voice that ran like a trickle of cold water down Bonnie's spine. "There's been enough killing, I say." It was a Union soldier with a double row of buttons on his jacket.

"More than enough," said another voice, like the boom of a faraway drum. A Confederate holding a bayonet.

"It's time somebody stopped it"—an old man in home-dyed butternut cloth.

"We can't let it go on"—the drummer boy with the black holes for eyes.

"No more blood spilled!" Several voices took it up at once. "No more killing!" The cry passed from one to another, until the swell of sound was louder than the roar of the fire. "No more blood!"

"*You can't touch me!* You can't kill me!"

"Let's take 'im, boys!"

Bonnie never knew who gave that last command. But he was obeyed by all, Confederate and Union soldiers alike. They were rising, flowing, dissolving into mist again, a dark mist with a hundred hands. It bore down on Klaus like an ocean wave, dashing itself on him and engulfing him. Each hand took hold, and although Klaus was fighting and thrashing with arms and legs, they were too many for him. In seconds he was obscured by them, surrounded, swallowed by the dark mist. It rose, whirling like a tornado from which screams could be heard only faintly.

"You can't kill me! I'm immortal!"

The tornado swept away into the darkness beyond Bonnie's sight. Following it was a trail of ghosts like a comet's tail, shooting off into the night sky.

"Where are they taking him?" Bonnie didn't mean to say it aloud; she just blurted it out before she thought. But Elena heard.

"Where he won't do any harm," she said, and the look on her face stopped Bonnie from asking any other questions.

There was a squealing, bleating sound from the other side of the clearing. Bonnie turned and saw Tyler, in his terrible part-human, part-animal shape, on his feet. There was no need for Caroline's club. He was staring at Elena and the few remaining ghostly figures and gibbering.

"Don't let them take me! Don't let them take me too!"

Before Elena could speak, he had spun around. He regarded the fire, which was higher than his own head, for an instant, then plunged right through it, crashing into the forest beyond. Through a parting of the flames, Bonnie saw him drop to the ground, beating out flames on himself, then rise and run again. Then the fire flared up and she couldn't see anything more.

But she'd remembered something: Meredith—and Matt. Meredith was lying propped up, her head in Caroline's lap, watching. Matt was still on his back. Hurt, but not so badly hurt as Stefan.

"Elena," Bonnie said, catching the bright figure's attention, and then she simply looked at him.

The brightness came closer. Stefan didn't blink. He looked into the heart of the light and smiled. "He's been stopped now. Thanks to you."

"It was Bonnie who called us. And she couldn't have done it at the right place and the right time without you and the others."

"I tried to keep my promise."

"I know, Stefan."

Bonnie didn't like the sound of this at all. It sounded too much like a farewell—a permanent one. Her own words floated back to her: *He might go to another place or—or just go out*. And she didn't want Stefan to go *anywhere*. Surely anyone who looked that much like an angel . . .

"Elena," she said, "can't you—do something? Can't you help him?" Her voice was shaking.

And Elena's expression as she turned to look at Bonnie, gentle but so sad, was even more distressing. It reminded her of someone, and then she remembered. Honoria Fell. Honoria's eyes had looked like that, as if she were looking at all the inescapable wrongs in the world. All the unfairness, all the things that shouldn't have been, but were.

"I can do something," she said. "But I don't know if it's the kind of help he wants." She turned back to Stefan. "Stefan, I can cure what Klaus did. Tonight I have that much Power. But I can't cure what Katherine did."

Bonnie's numbed brain struggled with this for a while. What Katherine did—but Stefan had recovered months ago from Katherine's torture in the crypt. Then she understood. What Katherine had done was make Stefan a vampire.

"It's been too long," Stefan was saying to Elena. "If you *did* cure it, I'd be a pile of dust."

"Yes." Elena didn't smile, just went on looking at him steadily. "Do you want my help, Stefan?"

"To go on living in this world in the shadows . . ." Stefan's voice was a whisper now, his green eyes distant. Bonnie wanted to shake him. *Live*, she thought to him, but she didn't dare say it for fear she'd make him decide just the opposite. Then she thought of something else.

"To go on trying," she said, and both of them looked at her. She looked back, chin thrust out, and saw the beginning of a smile on Elena's bright lips. Elena turned to Stefan, and that tiny hint of a smile passed to him.

"Yes," he said quietly, and then, to Elena, "I want your help."

She bent and kissed him.

Bonnie saw the brightness flow from her to Stefan, like a river of sparkling light engulfing him. It flooded over him the way the dark mist had surrounded Klaus, like a cascade of diamonds, until his entire body glowed like Elena's.

For an instant Bonnie imagined she could see the blood inside him turned molten, flowing out to each vein, each capillary, healing everything it touched. Then the glow faded to a golden aura, soaking back into Stefan's skin. His shirt was still demolished, but underneath the flesh was smooth and firm. Bonnie, feeling her own eyes wide with wonder, couldn't help reaching out to touch.

It felt just like any skin. The horrible wounds were gone.

She laughed aloud with sheer excitement, and then looked up, sobering. "Elena—there's Meredith, too—"

The bright being that was Elena was already moving across the clearing. Meredith looked up at her from Caroline's lap.

"Hello, Elena," she said, almost normally, except that her voice was so weak.

Elena bent and kissed her. The brightness flowed again, encompassing Meredith. And when it faded, Meredith stood up on her own two feet.

Then Elena did the same thing with Matt, who woke up, looking confused but alert. She kissed Caroline too, and Caroline stopped shaking and straightened.

Then she went to Damon.

He was still lying where he had fallen. The

ghosts had passed over him, taking no notice of him. Elena's brightness hovered over him, one shining hand reaching to touch his hair. Then she bent and kissed the dark head on the ground.

As the sparkling light faded, Damon sat up and shook his head. He saw Elena and went still, then, every movement careful and self-contained, stood up. He didn't say anything, only looked as Elena turned back to Stefan.

He was silhouetted against the fire. Bonnie had scarcely noticed how the red glow had grown so that it almost eclipsed Elena's gold. But now she saw it and felt a thrill of alarm.

"My last gift to you," Elena said, and it began to rain.

Not a thunder-and-lightning storm, but a thorough pattering rain that soaked everything —Bonnie included—and doused the fire. It was fresh and cool, and it seemed to wash all the horror of the last hours away, cleansing the glade of everything that had happened there. Bonnie tilted her face up to it, shutting her eyes, wanting to stretch out her arms and embrace it. At last it slackened and she looked again at Elena.

Elena was looking at Stefan, and there was no smile on her lips now. The wordless sorrow was back in her face.

"It's midnight," she said. "And I have to go."

Bonnie knew instantly, at the sound of it, that "go" didn't just mean for the moment. "Go" meant forever. Elena was going somewhere that no trance or dream could reach.

And Stefan knew it too.

"Just a few more minutes," he said, reaching for her.

"I'm sorry—"

"Elena, wait—I need to tell you—"

"I can't!" For the first time the serenity of that bright face was destroyed, showing not only gentle sadness but tearing grief. "Stefan, I can't wait. I'm so sorry." It was as if she were being pulled backward, retreating from them into some dimension that Bonnie could not see. Maybe the same place Honoria went when her task was finished, Bonnie thought. To be at peace.

But Elena's eyes didn't look as if she were at peace. They clung to Stefan, and she reached out her hand toward his, hopelessly. They didn't touch. Wherever Elena was being pulled was too far away.

"Elena—*please!*" It was the voice Stefan had called her with in his room. As if his heart was breaking.

"Stefan," she cried, both hands held out to him now. But she was diminishing, vanishing. Bonnie felt a sob swell in her own chest, close her own throat. It wasn't fair. All they had ever wanted was to be together. And now Elena's reward for helping the town and finishing her task was to be separated from Stefan irrevocably. It just wasn't *fair*.

"Stefan," Elena called again, but her voice came as if from a long distance. The brightness was almost gone. Then, as Bonnie stared through helpless tears, it winked out.

Leaving the clearing silent once again. They were all gone, the ghosts of Fell's Church who had walked for one night to keep more blood from being spilled. The bright spirit that had led them had vanished without a trace, and even the moon and stars were covered by clouds.

Bonnie knew that the wetness on Stefan's face wasn't due to the rain that was still splashing down.

He was standing, chest heaving, looking at the last place where Elena's brightness had been seen. And all the longing and the pain Bonnie had glimpsed on his face at times before was nothing to what she saw now.

"It isn't fair," she whispered. Then she shouted it to the sky, not caring who she was addressing. "It isn't fair!"

Stefan had been breathing more and more quickly. Now he lifted his face too, not in anger but in unbearable pain. His eyes were searching the clouds as if he might find some last trace of golden light, some flicker of brightness there. He couldn't. Bonnie saw the spasm go through him, like the agony of Klaus's stake. And the cry that burst out of him was the most terrible thing she'd ever heard.

"Elena!"

Sixteen

Bonnie never could quite remember how the next few seconds went. She heard Stefan's cry that almost seemed to shake the earth beneath her. She saw Damon start toward him. And then she saw the flash.

A flash like Klaus's lightning, only not blue-white. This one was gold.

And so bright Bonnie felt that the sun had exploded in front of her eyes. All she could make out for several seconds were whirling colors. And then she saw something in the middle of the clearing, near the chimney stack. Something white, shaped like the ghosts, only more solid looking. Something small and huddled that had to be anything but what her eyes were telling her it looked like.

Because it looked like a slender naked girl

trembling on the forest floor. A girl with golden hair.

It looked like Elena.

Not the glowing, candle-lit Elena of the spirit world and not the pale, inhumanly beautiful girl who had been Elena the vampire. This was an Elena whose creamy skin was blotching pink and showing gooseflesh under the spatter of the rain. An Elena who looked bewildered as she slowly raised her head and gazed around her, as if all the familiar things in the clearing were unfamiliar to her.

It's an illusion. Either that or they gave her a few minutes to say good-bye. Bonnie kept telling herself that, but she couldn't make herself believe it.

"Bonnie?" said a voice uncertainly. A voice that wasn't like wind chimes at all. The voice of a frightened young girl.

Bonnie's knees gave out. A wild feeling was growing inside her. She tried to push it away, not daring to even examine it yet. She just watched Elena.

Elena touched the grass in front of her. Hesitantly at first, then more and more firmly, quicker and quicker. She picked up a leaf in fingers that seemed clumsy, put it down, patted the ground. Snatched it up again. She grabbed a whole handful of wet leaves, held them to her, smelled them. She looked up at Bonnie, the leaves scattering away.

For a moment, they just knelt and stared at each other from the distance of a few feet. Then, tremulously, Bonnie stretched out her hand. She couldn't breathe. The feeling was growing and growing.

Elena's hand came up in turn. Reached toward Bonnie's. Their fingers touched.

Real fingers. In the real world. Where they both were.

Bonnie gave a kind of scream and threw herself on Elena.

In a minute she was patting her everywhere in a frenzy, with wild, disbelieving delight. And Elena was solid. She was wet from the rain and she was shivering and Bonnie's hands didn't go through her. Bits of damp leaf and crumbs of soil were clinging to Elena's hair.

"You're here," she sobbed. "I can touch you, Elena!"

Elena gasped back, "I can touch you! I'm here!" She grabbed the leaves again. "I can touch the ground!"

"I can see you touching it!" They might have kept this up indefinitely, but Meredith interrupted. She was standing a few steps away, staring, her dark eyes enormous, her face white. She made a choking sound.

"Meredith!" Elena turned to her and held out handfuls of leaves. She opened her arms.

Meredith, who had been able to cope when Elena's body was found in the river, when Elena had appeared at her window as a vampire, when Elena had materialized in the clearing like an angel, just stood there, shaking. She looked about to faint.

"Meredith, she's solid! You can touch her! See?" Bonnie pummeled Elena again joyfully.

Meredith didn't move. She whispered, "It's impossible—"

"It's true! See? It's true!" Bonnie was getting hysterical. She knew she was, and she didn't care. If anyone had a right to get hysterical, it was her. "It's true, it's true," she caroled. "Meredith, come *see*."

Meredith, who had been staring at Elena all this while, made another choked sound. Then, with one motion, she flung herself down on Elena. She touched her, found that her hand met the resistance of flesh. She looked into Elena's face. And then she burst into uncontrollable tears.

She cried and cried, her head on Elena's naked shoulder.

Bonnie gleefully patted both of them.

"Don't you think she'd better put something on?" said a voice, and Bonnie looked up to see

Caroline taking off her dress. Caroline did it rather calmly, standing in her beige polyester slip afterward as if she did this sort of thing all the time. No imagination, Bonnie thought again, but without malice. Clearly there were times when no imagination was an advantage.

Meredith and Bonnie pulled the dress over Elena's head. She looked small inside it, wet and somehow unnatural, as if she wasn't used to clothing anymore. But it was some protection from the elements, anyway.

Then Elena whispered, "Stefan."

She turned. He was standing there, with Damon and Matt, a little apart from the girls. He was just watching her. As if not only his breath, but his life was held, waiting.

Elena got up and took a tottery step to him, and then another and another. Slim and newly fragile inside her borrowed dress, she wavered as she moved toward him. Like the little mermaid learning how to use her legs, Bonnie thought.

He let her get almost all the way there, just staring, before he stumbled toward her. They ended in a rush and then fell to the ground together, arms locked around each other, each holding on as tightly as possible. Neither of them said a word.

At last Elena pulled back to look at Stefan, and he cupped her face between his hands, just gazing back at her. Elena laughed aloud for sheer joy, opening and closing her own fingers and looking at them in delight before burying them in Stefan's hair. Then they kissed.

Bonnie watched unabashedly, feeling some of the heady joy spill over into tears. Her throat ached, but these were sweet tears, not the salt tears of pain, and she was still smiling. She was filthy, she was soaking wet, she had never been so happy in her life. She felt as if she wanted to dance and sing and do all sorts of crazy things.

Some time later Elena looked up from Stefan to all of them, her face almost as bright as when she'd floated in the clearing like an angel. Shining like starlight. No one will ever call her Ice Princess again, Bonnie thought.

"My friends," Elena said. It was all she said, but it was enough, that and the queer little sob she gave as she held out a hand to them. They were around her in a second, swarming her, all trying to embrace at once. Even Caroline.

"Elena," Caroline said, "I'm sorry . . ."

"It's all forgotten now," Elena said, and hugged her as freely as anyone else. Then she grasped a sturdy brown hand and held it briefly to her cheek. "Matt," she said, and he smiled at her, blue eyes swimming. But not with misery at seeing her in Stefan's arms, Bonnie thought. Just now Matt's face expressed only happiness.

A shadow fell over the little group, coming between them and the moonlight. Elena looked up, and held out her hand again.

"Damon," she said.

The clear light and shining love in her face was irresistible. Or it should have been irresistible, Bonnie thought. But Damon stepped forward unsmiling, his black eyes as bottomless and unfathomable as ever. None of the starlight that shone from Elena was reflected back from them.

Stefan looked up at him fearlessly, as he'd looked into the painful brilliance of Elena's golden brightness. Then, never looking away, he held out his hand as well.

Damon stood gazing down at them, the two open, fearless faces, the mute offer of their hands. The offer of connection, warmth, humanity. Nothing showed in his own face, and he was utterly motionless himself.

"Come on, Damon," Matt said softly. Bonnie looked at him quickly, and saw that the blue eyes were intent now as they looked at the shadowed hunter's face.

Damon spoke without moving. "I'm not like you."

"You're not as different from us as you want to think," Matt said. "Look," he added, an odd note of challenge in his voice, "I know you killed Mr. Tanner in self-defense, because you told me. And I know you didn't come here to Fell's Church because Bonnie's spell dragged you here, because I sorted the hair and I didn't make any mistakes. You're more like us than you admit, Damon. The only thing I *don't* know is why you didn't go into Vickie's house to help her."

Damon snapped, almost automatically, "Because I wasn't invited!"

Memory swept over Bonnie. Herself standing outside Vickie's house, Damon standing beside her. Stefan's voice: *Vickie, invite me in*. But no one had invited Damon.

"But how did *Klaus* get in, then—?" she began, following her own thoughts.

"That was Tyler's job, I'm sure," Damon said tersely. "What Tyler did for Klaus in return for learning how to reclaim his heritage. And he must have invited Klaus in before we ever started guarding the house—probably before Stefan and I came to Fell's Church. Klaus was well prepared. That night he was in the house and the girl was dead before I knew what was happening."

"Why didn't you call for Stefan?" Matt said. There was no accusation in his voice. It was a simple question.

"Because there was nothing he could have done! *I* knew what you were dealing with as soon as I saw it. An Old One. Stefan would only have gotten himself killed—and the girl was past caring, anyway."

Bonnie heard the thread of coldness in his voice, and when Damon turned back to Stefan and Elena, his face had hardened. It was as if some decision had been made.

"You see, I'm not like you," he said.

"It doesn't matter." Stefan had still not withdrawn his hand. Neither had Elena.

"And sometimes the good guys *do* win," Matt said quietly, encouragingly.

"Damon—" Bonnie began. Slowly, almost reluctantly, he turned toward her. She was thinking about that moment when they had been kneeling over Stefan and he had looked so young. When they had been just Damon and Bonnie at the edge of the world.

She thought, for just one instant, that she saw stars in those black eyes. And she could sense in him something—some ferment of feelings like longing and confusion and fear and anger all mixed. But then it was all smoothed over again and his shields were back up and Bonnie's psychic senses told her nothing. And those black eyes were simply opaque.

He turned back to the couple on the ground. Then he removed his jacket and stepped behind Elena. He draped it over her shoulders without touching her.

"It's a cold night," he said. His eyes held Stefan's a moment as he settled the black jacket around her.

And then he turned to walk into the darkness between the oak trees. In an instant Bonnie heard the rush of wings.

Stefan and Elena wordlessly joined hands again, and Elena's golden head dropped to Stefan's shoulder. Over her hair Stefan's green eyes were turned toward the patch of night where his brother had disappeared.

Bonnie shook her head, feeling a catch in her throat. It was eased as something touched her arm and she looked up at Matt. Even soaking wet, even covered with bits of moss and fern, he was a beautiful sight. She smiled at him, feeling her wonder and joy come back. The giddy, dizzy excitement as she thought about what had happened tonight. Meredith and Caroline were smiling too, and in an impulsive burst Bonnie seized Matt's hands and whirled him into a dance. In the middle of the clearing they kicked up wet leaves and spun and laughed. They were alive, and they were young, and it was the summer solstice.

"You wanted us all back together again!" Bonnie shouted at Caroline, and pulled the scandalized girl into the dance. Meredith, her dignity forgotten, joined them too.

And for a long time in the clearing there was only rejoicing.

June 21, 7:30 a.m.
The Summer Solstice
Dear Diary,

Oh, it's all too much to explain and you wouldn't believe it anyway. I'm going to bed.

Bonnie

Don't miss L. J. Smith's next terrifying trilogy:

The Secret Circle

Volume I: The Initiation

Chapter One

It wasn't supposed to be this hot and humid on Cape Cod. Cassie had seen it in the guide book; everything was supposed to be perfect here, like Camelot.

Except, the guidebook added absently, for the poison ivy, and ticks, and green flies, and toxic shellfish, and undercurrents in seemingly peaceful water.

The book had also warned against hiking out on narrow peninsulas, because high tide could come along and strand you. But, just at this moment, Cassie would have given anything to be stranded on some peninsula jutting far out into the Atlantic Ocean—as long as Portia Bainbridge was on the other side.

Cassie had never been so miserable in her life.

". . . and my other brother, the one on the MIT debate team, the one who went to the World Debate Tournament in Scotland two years ago . . ." Portia was saying. Cassie felt her eyes glaze over again and slipped back into her wretched trance.

Just one more week, Cassie told herself. Just one more week and I can go home. The very thought filled her with a longing so sharp that tears came to her eyes. Home, where her friends were. Where she didn't feel like a stranger, and unaccomplished, and boring, and stupid just because she didn't know what a quahog was. Where she could laugh about all this: her wonderful vacation on the eastern seaboard.

". . . so my father said, 'Why don't I just *buy* it for you?' But I said, 'No—well, maybe . . .' "

Cassie stared out at the sea.

It wasn't that the Cape wasn't beautiful. The little cedar-shingled cottages and the village greens and tall-steepled churches and old-fashioned schoolhouses made Cassie feel as if she'd stepped into a different time.

But every day there was Portia to deal with. And far worse was the plain raw feeling of *not belonging*. Of being a stranger here, stranded on the wrong coast, completely out of her own element.

One more week, she thought. You can stand anything for one more week.

And then there was Mom, so pale lately and so quiet. . . . A worried twinge went through Cassie and she quickly pushed it away. Mom is fine, she told herself fiercely. She's probably just miserable here, the same way you are, even though this is her native state. She's probably counting the days until we can go home, just like you are. Everything would be all right when they got back home, for both of them.

"Cassie are you *listening* to me?"

Cassie jumped. "Of course. Sure."

"What did I just say?"

Cassie floundered. Boyfriends, she thought desperately, the debate team, college . . . but Portia was already talking again.

"I was saying they shouldn't let people like that on the beach, especially not with dogs. I mean, I know this isn't Oyster Harbor, but at least it's clean. And now look." Cassie looked, following the direction of Portia's gaze. All she could see was some guy walking down the beach. She looked back at Portia uncertainly.

"He works on a *fishing* boat," Portia said. Her nostrils flared as if she smelled something bad. "I saw him this morning on the fish pier, unloading. I don't think he's even changed his *clothes*. How totally scuzzy."

He didn't look scuzzy to Cassie. He had dark red hair, and he was tall, and even at this distance she could see that he was smiling. There was a dog at his heels.

"We never talk to guys from the fishing boats. We don't even look at them," Portia said. And Cassie could see it was true. There were maybe a dozen other girls on the beach, in groups of two or three, a few with guys, most not. As the tall boy passed, the girls would look away, turning their heads to stare in the opposite direction. As the guy got closer to her, Cassie could see that his smile was turning grim.

The two girls closest to Cassie and Portia were looking away now, almost sniffing. Cassie saw the boy shrug slightly as if it were no more than he expected. She still didn't see anything disgusting about him. He was wearing ragged cut-off shorts and a T-shirt that had seen better days, but lots of guys looked like that. And his dog trotted right behind him, tail waving, friendly and alert. It wasn't bothering anybody. Cassie glanced up at the boy's face, curious to see his eyes.

"Look *down*," Portia whispered. The guy was passing right in front of them. Cassie hastily looked down, obeying automatically, although she felt a surge of rebellion in her heart. It seemed cheap and nasty and unnecessary and cruel, she thought. She was ashamed to be a part of it, but she couldn't help doing what Portia said.

She stared at her fingers trailing into the sand. *Unfair*, she thought to the boy, who of course couldn't hear her. *I'm sorry; this just isn't fair. I wish I could do something, but I can't.*

A wet nose thrust under her hand.

The suddenness of it made her gasp, and a giggle caught in her throat, barely choked down. The dog pushed at her hand again—not asking, demanding. Cassie petted it, scratching at the short silky-bristly hairs on its nose. It was a German shepherd, a big handsome dog with liquid, intelligent brown eyes and a laughing mouth. Cassie felt the stiff, embarrassed mask she'd been wearing break and she laughed back at it.

Then she glanced up at the dog's owner, quickly, unable to help herself. She met his eyes directly.

Later, Cassie would think of that moment, the moment when she looked up at him and he looked down at her. His eyes were blue-gray, like the sea at its most mysterious. His face was arresting and intriguing, with high cheekbones and a determined mouth. Proud and independent and humorous and sensitive all at once. As he looked down at her, his grim smile lightened and something sparkled in those blue-gray eyes, like sun glinting off the waves. It was like a rainbow coming out, irresistible.

Normally Cassie was shy around guys, especially guys she didn't know, but she felt sorry for this guy, and she wanted to be nice. Besides, she couldn't help it. And so when she felt herself start to sparkle back at him, her laughter bubbling up in response to his smile, she let it happen. In that instant it was as if they were sharing a secret, something nobody else on the beach could understand. The dog wiggled ecstatically as if he were in on it, too.

"*Cassie*," came Portia's fuming hiss.

Cassie felt herself turn red and she snatched her eyes away from the guy's face. Portia was looking apoplectic.

"Raj!" the boy said, not laughing anymore. "Heel!"

With apparent reluctance, the dog backed away from Cassie, tail still wagging. Then, in a spray of sand, he bounded toward his master. Cassie couldn't keep her eyes down any longer. She glanced up again, quickly and apologetically, and found the boy looking straight at her once more. His eyes were now as dark as the sea in a storm.

And then he was walking away, the dog frisking behind him. He didn't look back.

Cassie's thoughts were shattered by a hiss at her side. She cringed, knowing exactly what Portia was going to say. That the dog probably had mange and fleas and worms and scrofula.

But Portia didn't say it. She too was staring after the retreating figures of the boy and dog as they went up a dune, along a little path in the beach grass. And although she was clearly disgusted, there was something else in her face—a sort of dark speculation and suspicion that Cassie had never seen there before.

"What's the matter, Portia?"

Portia's eyes had narrowed. "I think," she said

slowly, through tight lips, "that I've seen him before."

"You already said so. You saw him on the fish pier."

Portia shook her head impatiently. "Not *that*. Shut up and let me think."

Stunned, Cassie shut up.

Portia continued to stare, and after a few moments she began nodding, little nods to confirm something to herself. Her face was blotched red, and not with sunburn.

Abruptly, she muttered something and stood up.

"Portia?"

"I've got to do something," Portia said, waving a hand at Cassie without looking at her. "You stay here."

"What's going *on*?"

"Nothing!" Portia glanced at her sharply. "Nothing's going on. Just forget all about it. I'll see you later." She walked off, moving quickly, heading up the dunes toward the cottage her family owned.

Forget all about what? Cassie felt stung and sore—even Portia had never been this rude before. And besides, she didn't understand. Where did Portia think she'd seen that guy before? And what was she going to do that she didn't want Cassie along?

She should have been deliriously happy just to have Portia leave her alone, for any reason. But now Cassie found she couldn't enjoy it. Her mind was all churned up, like the choppy water before a gale. She felt agitated and distressed and almost frightened.

The strangest thing was what Portia had muttered before getting up. It had been under her breath, and Cassie didn't think she could have heard it right. It must have been something else, like "snitch," or "bitch," or "rich."

She *must* have heard it wrong. You wouldn't call a *guy* a witch, for God's sake.

Calm down, she told herself. Don't worry, be happy. You're alone at last.

But she couldn't relax. She stood and picked up her towel. Then, wrapping it around her, she started down the beach the way the guy had gone.

Chapter Two

When Cassie got to the place where the boy had turned, she walked up the dunes between the pitiful little clumps of scraggly beach grass. At the top she looked around, but there was nothing to be seen but pitch pines and scrub oak trees. No boy. No dog. Silence.

She was hot.

All right, fine. She turned back toward the sea. She'd go get wet and cool off. Portia's problem was Portia's problem. As for the red-haired guy—well, she'd probably never see him again, and he wasn't her business either.

A little inside shiver went through her; not the kind that shows, but the kind that makes you wonder if you're sick. I must be *too* hot, she realized; hot enough that it starts to feel cold. I need a dip in the water. The water was cool because this was the open Atlantic side of the Cape. She didn't go all the way in, but waded up to her knees and then continued walking down the beach, farther away from Portia's towel every minute.

When she reached a dock, she splashed out of the water and climbed up to it. Only three boats were tied up there; two rowboats and a powerboat. It was deserted.

It was just what Cassie needed.

She unhooked the thick, frayed rope meant to keep people like her off the dock and walked onto it. She walked far out, the weatherbeaten wood creaking beneath her feet, the water stretching out on either side of her. When she looked back at the beach she saw there wasn't a person in sight. A little breeze blew in her face, stirring her hair and making her wet legs tingle. Suddenly she felt—she couldn't explain it—like a balloon caught in the wind and lifted, sailing off toward strange new places, undiscovered lands. She felt light, she felt expanded. She felt free. She smiled as she got to the end of the dock and sat down.

The sky and the ocean were exactly the same deep jewel-blue, except that the sky lightened down at the horizon where they met. Cassie thought that she could see the curve of the earth, but it might have been her imagination. Terns and herring gulls were wheeling above and she wondered what it looked like from their point of view.

But it was lovely just to be where she was, lovely to be alone, lovely to smell the salt sea-smell and to feel the warm planks beneath her and to hear the soft splashing of the water against the wooden pilings.

It was a hypnotic sound, rhythmic as a giant heartbeat or the breathing of the planet. Cassie sat and gazed and listened, and as she did she felt her own breathing slow. For the first time since she'd come to New England, she felt she belonged.

Staring out to sea, she felt words come to her. Just a little jingle, like something you'd teach a child, but a poem nonetheless.

Sky and sea, keep harm from me.

The strange thing was that it didn't feel like something she'd made up. It felt more like something she'd read—or heard?—a long time ago. She had a brief flash of an image: being held in someone's arms and looking at the ocean. Being held up high and hearing words.

Sky and sea, keep harm from me. Earth and fire, bring . . .

No.

Shocked, Cassie felt her thoughts pull up short. Her skin was tingling.

Don't finish it, she thought. Don't say any more. A sudden irrational conviction had taken hold of her. As long as she didn't go on, didn't find the last words of the poem, she was safe. Everything would be as it always had been, she would go home and live out her quiet, ordinary life in peace.

But the poem was running through her mind, like the tinkling of icy music far away, and the last words fell into place. She couldn't stop them.

Sky and sea, keep harm from me. Earth and fire, bring my desire.

Yes.

Oh, what have I *done?*

It was like a string snapping, like the surge and crest of a great wave over her. Cassie found herself on her feet, staring wildly out at the ocean. Something had happened then. She had felt it.

She no longer felt light and free, but jangled and out of tune and full of static electricity. As if *something* had been started and couldn't be stopped now. Turning sharply, she headed back toward the shore.

Idiot, she thought as she neared the white sand of the beach again, and the frightening feelings slipped away. What were you afraid of? That the sky and the sea were really listening to you? That those words were actually going to *do* something?

She could almost laugh at it now, and she was embarrassed and annoyed with herself. Talk about an overactive imagination. Words were only words.

But then a movement caught her eye, and she would always remember that deep down she had not been surprised.

Something *was* happening. There was motion on the shore.

It was the red-haired guy and his dog. He'd burst out between the pitch pines and was running down the slope of a dune. Suddenly inexplicably calm,

Cassie hurried the rest of the way down the dock to meet him as he reached the sand.

The guy looked right and left, up and down the deserted beach. A hundred yards to the left a headland jutted out so you couldn't see what was beyond. Without even glancing at Cassie, he started that way.

Cassie's heart was beating hard.

"Wait," she said urgently.

He turned, scanning her quickly with his blue-gray eyes.

"Who's after you?" she said, even though she thought she knew already.

"Two guys who look like linebackers for the *New York Giants*."

Cassie nodded, feeling the thump of her heart accelerate. But her voice was still calm. "Their names are Jordan and Logan Bainbridge."

"It figures."

"You've heard of them?"

"No. But it figures they'd be named something like that."

Cassie almost laughed. She liked the way he looked, so windblown and alert, scarcely out of breath even though he'd been running hard. And she liked the daredevil sparkle in his eyes and the way he joked even though he was in trouble.

"Raj and I could take them, but they've got a couple of friends with them," he said, turning again. Walking backward, he added, "You'd better go the other way—you don't want to run into them. And it would be nice if you could pretend you hadn't seen me."

"Wait!" cried Cassie.

Whatever was going on wasn't her business, and she shouldn't be getting mixed up in it . . . but she found herself speaking without hesitation. There was something about this guy; something that made her want to help him. That *compelled* her to help him.

"That way's a dead end—around the headland you'll run into rocks. You'll be trapped."

"But the other way's too straight."

Cassie's thoughts were flying, and then suddenly she knew. "Hide in the boat."

"What?"

"In the *boat*. In the powerboat. On the dock." She gestured at it. "You can get in the cabin and they won't see you."

His eyes followed hers, but he shook his head. "I'd really be trapped if they found me there. And Raj doesn't like to swim."

"They won't find you," Cassie said. "They won't go near it. I'll tell them you went down the beach that way."

He stared at her, the smile dying out of his eyes. "You don't understand," he said quietly. "Those guys are trouble."

"I don't *care*," Cassie said, and she almost

pushed him toward the dock. She didn't care. All that mattered was that he got out of sight.

"But—"

"Oh, *please*. Don't argue. Just do it!"

He stared at her one last instant, then turned, slapping his thigh for the dog. "C'mon, boy!" He ran down the dock and jumped easily into the powerboat, disappearing as he ducked into the cabin. The dog followed him in one powerful spring and barked.

Shh! thought Cassie. The two in the boat were hidden now, but if anyone went up the dock they would be plainly visible. She hooked the loop of frayed rope over the top of the last piling again, screening off the dock once more. Then she thought fast. What should she be doing? She didn't want to draw attention to the dock, so what should she be doing out here?

She cast a frantic glance around, then headed for the water, splashing in. Bending down, she dug up a handful of wet sand and shells.

She heard shouting from the dunes.

I'm gathering shells. I'm only gathering shells. I don't need to look up yet. I'm not concerned.

"Hey!"

Cassie looked up.

There were four of them, and the two in front were Portia's brothers. Jordan was the one on the debate team and Logan was the one in the Pistol Club. Or was it the other way around?

"Hey, did you see a guy come running this way?" Jordan asked. They were looking in all directions, excited like dogs on a scent, and suddenly another line of poetry came to Cassie. *Four lean hounds crouched low and smiling.* Except that these guys weren't lean; they were brawny and sweaty. And out of breath, Cassie noticed, vaguely triumphant.

"It's Portia's friend—Cathy," said Logan. "Hey, Cathy, did a guy just go running down here?"

Cassie walked toward him slowly, her fists full of shells. Her heart was knocking against her ribs so hard she was sure they could see it, and her tongue was frozen.

"Can't you talk? What're you doing here?"

Mutely, Cassie held out her hands, opening them.

They exchanged glances and snorts, and suddenly Cassie knew how she must look to these college-age guys—a silly little high school ditz from out of state whose idea of a good time was picking up worthless shells.

"Did you see somebody go *past* here?" Jordan said, impatient but slow, as if she might be hard of hearing.

Dry-mouthed, Cassie nodded, and looked down the beach toward the headland. Jordan was wearing an open windbreaker over his T-shirt, which seemed odd in such warm weather. What was even odder was the bulge beneath it, but when he turned, Cassie saw the glint of metal.

A *gun*?

Jordan must be the one in the Pistol Club, she thought irrelevantly.

Now that she saw something to really be scared about, she found her voice again and said huskily, "A guy and a dog went that way a few minutes ago." To clinch it, she added, "It was the same guy who went by Portia and me on the beach."

"We've got him! He'll be stuck on the rocks!" Logan said. He and the two guys Cassie didn't know started down the beach, but Jordan turned back to Cassie.

"Are you sure?"

Startled, she looked up at him. Why was he asking? She deliberately widened her eyes and tried to look as childish and stupid as possible. "Yes . . ."

"It's *important*." And suddenly he was holding her wrist. Cassie looked down at it in amazement, her shells scattering, too surprised at being grabbed to say anything. "It's very important," Jordan said, and she could feel the tension running through his body, could smell the acridity of his sweat. A wave of revulsion swept through her and she struggled to keep her face blank and wide-eyed. She was afraid he was going to pull her up against him, but he just twisted her wrist.

She didn't mean to cry out, but she did anyway. It was partly pain and partly a reaction to something she saw in his eyes, something fanatical and ugly and hot like fire. She found herself gasping, more afraid than she could remember being since she was a child. And he's got a gun, she thought stupidly.

"Yes, I'm sure," she said, breathless, staring into that ugliness without letting herself look away. "He went down there and around the headland."

"Come on, Jordan, leave her alone," Logan shouted. "She's just a kid. Let's go!"

Jordan hesitated.

He knows I'm lying, Cassie thought, with a curious fascination, and her stomach seemed to plummet.

Believe me, she thought, gazing straight back at him, willing him to do it. Believe me and go away. *Believe me.*

He let go of her wrist.

"Sorry," he muttered ungraciously, and he turned around and loped off with the others.

Tingling, Cassie watched them jog across the wet sand, elbows and knees pumping, Jordan's windbreaker flapping loose behind him. The weakness spread from her stomach to her legs, and her knees suddenly felt like Silly Putty.

When the four running figures turned the corner, disappearing from her sight, she turned back to the dock, meaning to tell the red-haired guy that he could come out now.

He already had.

Slowly, she made her jellied legs carry her to the

dock. He was just standing there, and the look on his face made her feel strange.

"You'd better get out of here—or maybe hide again," she said hesitantly. "They might come right back . . ."

"I don't think so."

"Well . . ." Cassie faltered, looking at him, feeling almost frightened. "Your dog was very good," she offered uncertainly, at last. "I mean, keeping still like that. Not barking."

"He knows better."

"Oh." Cassie looked down the beach, trying to think of something else to say. His voice was gentle, not harsh, but that keen look never left his eyes and his mouth was grim. "I guess they really are gone now," she said.

"Thanks to you," he said. He turned to her and their eyes met. "I don't know how to thank you," he added, "for putting up with that for me. Why would you do something like that for a stranger? You don't even know me."

Cassie felt even more queer. Looking up at him made her almost dizzy, but she couldn't take her eyes from his. There was no sparkle now, they looked like blue-gray steel. Compelling. Hypnotic. Drawing her closer, drawing her in.

But I do know you, she thought. In that instant a strange image flashed through her mind. It was as if she were floating outside herself and she could see the two of them, standing there on the beach. She could see the sun shining on his hair and her face tilted up to him. And they were connected by a silver cord which hummed and sang with power.

A band of energy linking them, tying them together. It was so real, she could almost reach out and touch it. She could feel its force. But in that same giddy instant she saw that they were only two points of a triangle. The silver cord was connected to something else, something she couldn't see. *I've known you before*, she thought. *I have always known you. And we have both known—another. Who . . . ?*

Suddenly, as quickly as it had come, the picture vanished. She blinked and shook her head, trying to wrench her mind back from what she'd seen—what she'd imagined she had seen. He was still looking at her, waiting for an answer to his question.

"I was glad to help you," she said, feeling how lame and inadequate the words were. "And I didn't mind—what happened." His eyes dropped to her wrist and there was a flash from them almost like silver.

"I *did*," he said. "I should have come out earlier."

Cassie shook her head again. The last thing she'd wanted was for him to be caught and hurt. "I just wanted to help you," she repeated softly, confused. Then she said, "Why were they chasing you?"

He looked away, drawing in a deep breath. Cassie sensed that she was trespassing. "That's all right. I shouldn't have asked—" she began.

"They don't like people who are—different," he said, his voice quiet. "And I'm different from them. I'm very, very different."

Yes, she thought. Whatever he was, he wasn't like Jordan or Logan. He wasn't like anyone she had ever met.

"I'm sorry. That's not much of an explanation, I know," he said. "Especially after what you did. You did help me, and I won't forget about it." He glanced down at himself and laughed shortly. "Of course, it doesn't look like there's much *I* can do for *you*, does it? Not here. Although . . ." He paused. "Wait a minute."

He reached in his pocket, fingers groping for something. All in an instant Cassie's dizziness overwhelmed her, blood rushing to her face. Was he looking for money? Did he think he could *pay* her for helping him? She was humiliated, and more stricken than when Jordan had grabbed her wrist, and she couldn't help the tears flooding her eyes.

But what he pulled out of his pocket was a stone, a rock like something you might pick up off the ocean floor. At least that was what it looked like at first to Cassie. One side was rough and gray, embedded with tiny black spirals like little shells. But then he turned it over, and the other side was gray swirled with pale blue, crystallized, sparkling in the sunlight as if it was overlaid with rock candy. It was beautiful.

He pressed it into her palm, closing her fingers around it. As it touched her, she felt a jolt of electricity run through her hand and up her arm. The stone felt *alive* in some way she couldn't explain. Through the pounding in her ears she heard him speaking, quickly and in a low voice, utterly serious.

"This is chalcedony. It's a—good luck piece. If you're ever in trouble or danger or anything like that, if there's ever a time when you feel all alone and no one else can help you, hold onto it tight. *Tight*." His fingers squeezed hers—"and think of me."

She stared up at him, mesmerized. She was hardly breathing and her chest felt too full, her heart echoing as if it were underwater. He was so close to her; she could see his eyes, the same color as the crystal, and she could feel his breath on her skin, and the warmth of his body reflecting the sun's heat. His hair wasn't just red, but all sorts of colors, some strands so dark they were almost purple, others like burgundy wine, others almost gold.

Different, she thought again; he was different from any guy she'd ever known. A sweet hot current was running through her, a feeling of wildness and possibility. She was trembling and she could feel a heartbeat in her fingers, but she couldn't tell if it was hers or his. He was so close and he was looking down at her . . .

"And what happens then?" she whispered.

"And then—maybe your luck will change." Abruptly he stepped back, as if he'd just remembered something, and his tone had altered. The moment was over. "It's worth a try, don't you think?" he said lightly.

Unable to speak, she nodded. He was teasing now. But he hadn't been before.

"I've got to go now. I shouldn't have stayed this long," he said.

Cassie swallowed. "You'd better be careful. I think Jordan had a gun—"

"Wouldn't surprise me." He brushed it off, stopping her from saying anything further. "Don't worry; I'm leaving the Cape. For now, anyway. But I'll be back. Maybe I'll see you then." He started to turn. Then he paused one last moment and took her hand again. Cassie was too startled by the feeling of his skin against hers to do anything about it. He turned her hand over and looked at the red marks on her wrist, then brushed them lightly with his fingertips. The steely light was back in his eyes when he looked up. "And believe me," he whispered. "Believe me; he'll pay for this someday. I guarantee it."

And then he did something which shocked Cassie more than anything else during that whole shocking day. He lifted her wounded hand to his lips and kissed it. It was the gentlest, the lightest of touches, and it went through Cassie like fire. She stared at him, dazed and unbelieving, utterly speechless. She could neither move nor think. She could only stand there and *feel.*

And then he was leaving, whistling for the dog which romped around Cassie in circles before finally breaking away. She was left alone, gazing after him, her fingers clenched tightly on the small rough stone in her palm.

It was only then she realized she'd never asked him his name.